ELF GIRL AND RAVEN BOY:
FRIGHT FOREST

ELF GIRL AND RAVEN BOY:
FRIGHT FOREST

Marcus Sedgwick

Illustrated by Pete Williamson

First published in 2012
by Orion Children's Books,
a division of the Orion Publishing
Group Ltd
This Large Print edition published by
AudioGO Ltd 2013
by arrangement with
the Orion Publishing Group Ltd

ISBN: 978 1471 320170

British Library Cataloguing in Publication Data available

Printed and bound in Great Britain by
MPG Books Group Limited

For small forest creatures
everywhere . . .

Scream Sea

The Island

Monster Mountains

Fright Forest

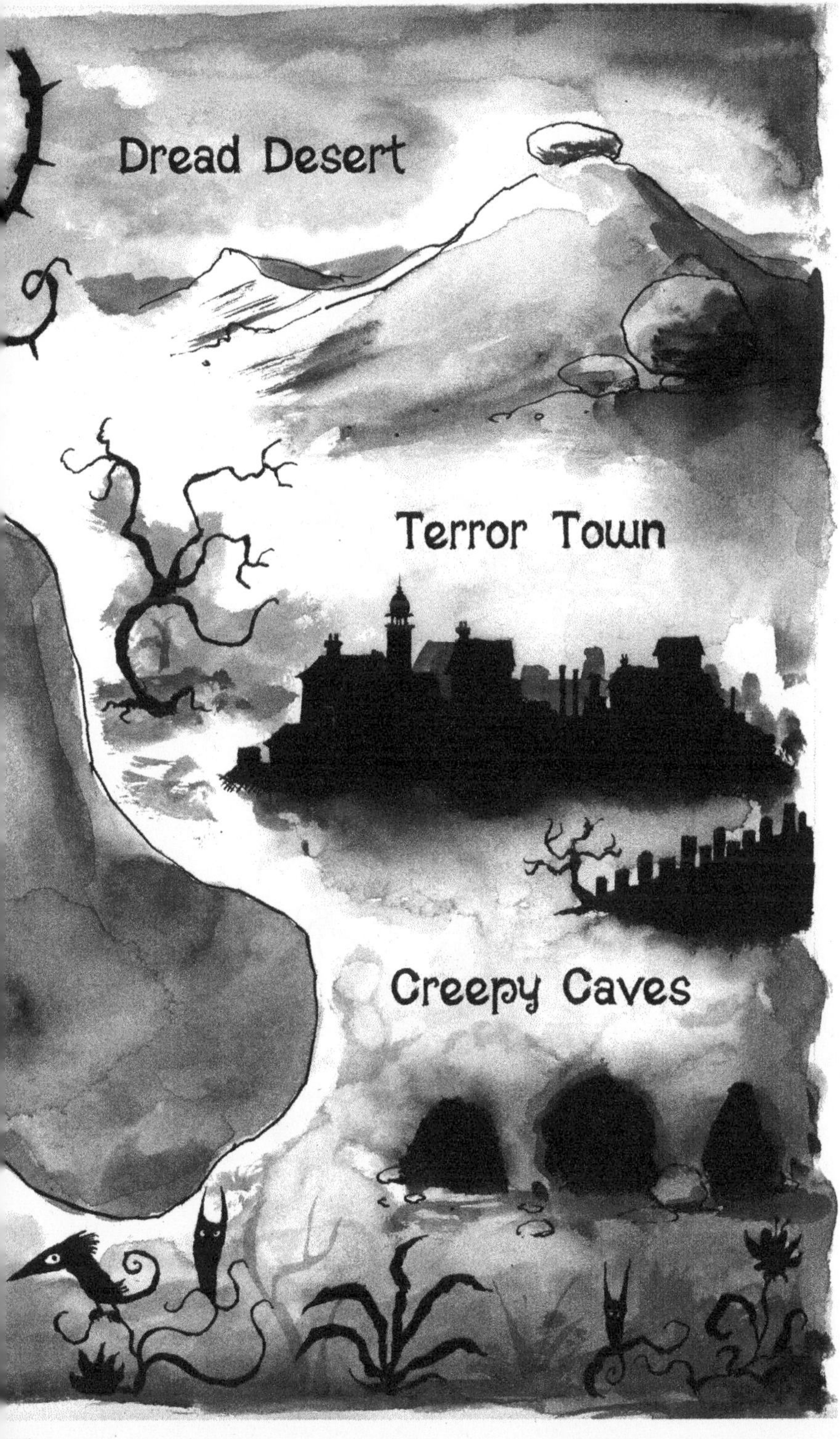
Dread Desert
Terror Town
Creepy Caves

ONE

Raven Boy is *so* good at climbing trees that he goes higher even than really brave squirrels do.

When Raven Boy met Elf Girl, he was not called Raven Boy, and she was not called Elf Girl. Not then.

1

On the night they met, Raven Boy, as he would soon be known, was as usual sleeping happily in the top of a tall tree, the tallest he could find. It was the middle of the night, and the endless forest was quiet. No bats darted here and there, no owls hooted spookily, nothing rustled in the slightest.

It was quiet in a something-really-bad-is-about-to-happen way.

And then, strangely enough, something really bad did happen.

The tree in which Raven Boy was sleeping began to sway. Just a little bit at first, so he didn't wake up. He was dreaming about baby squirrels and he had a smile on his face.

Then the treetop swayed some more, a lot more, which was odd because there wasn't even the gentlest of breezes. It was swaying because it was falling down.

Raven Boy's eyes shot open.

'Eep!' he screeched and began grabbing at branches, but even with his amazing climbing skills, it was hopeless. The tree was hurtling towards the ground, smashing through the branches of other trees as it went.

He heard the loud squawk of birds and the terrible noise of the trunk splitting, and a second or two later, the tree smashed onto the forest floor. It was all he could do to jump at the last minute, and by chance he found himself hanging from a branch near the ground.

'Eep,' he said again, his eyes as wide as dinner plates.

He dangled for a bit, then felt stupid, even though it was the middle of the night and he knew no one could see him.

'Who are you?' said a voice. 'And why are you dangling in that tree? You look stupid. And why?' the voice sounded quite cross now, 'have you squashed my hut?'

The boy who would very soon be known as Raven Boy looked around. He

4

had incredibly good night vision, so although it was dark, he saw the girl who'd spoken to him.

'Who are you?' he said.

'I asked you first,' replied a rather tiny and skinny girl.

'So?'

'So, what?'

'So you tell me your name first.'

'Is that how it works?'

'Yes,' said the girl. 'It is.'

He thought about this.

'No,' he said.

'No? No what?'

'No, I won't tell you my name.'

'Why not?' asked the girl.

He had two reasons for this; the first was that he had a really silly name and he was very embarrassed about it, the second was that he was about to slip from the tree.

'Eep!' he said, and landed on the girl.

She rolled out from under him and stood up. She was so cross she put her hands on her hips and her ears turned pink. Then she pointed at him.

5

'You!' she said. 'Why are you covered in feathers?'

'I fell through a bird nest on the way down.'

That was true, but the fact is that he often had a feather or two poking out from his hair, or from his tattered coat—that's what happens when you spend most of your time in treetops. You pick things up. Feathers, pine cones, leaves. Small creatures.

'You look more like a raven than a boy,' she said, laughing. Then she stopped laughing. 'Oh! Look at my hut!'

'What hut?'

The girl pointed at the tree trunk, from underneath which a splinter of roof poked out.

'You've flattened my home!'

'I didn't do . . .'

'What was that?'

She pricked up her ears, which he noticed were rather pointy. He'd heard the noise too.

'It's another tree! And it's coming this way!'

'Run, Raven Boy! Run!'

They ran, but not far enough. Because it was dark and they were a bit stupid, they didn't run to the side, but straight ahead, so that when the tree hit the ground, its topmost branches bopped them both and that was that.

Flattened, or very nearly, they were only saved because they'd fallen into a large badger hole at the last moment.

By the time they woke up again, it was morning.

Sun beams were peeking around the tree trunk and down into the badger hole.

Raven Boy blinked, totally forgetting what had happened for a minute. Then he looked about him, at the badger hole, the tree above him, and at the skinny girl sitting next to him, picking leaves and the odd worm out of her hair.

'Why are your ears pointy?' asked

Raven Boy.

'Same reason your nose is, I suppose.'

Raven Boy thought about this.

'You still have feathers in your hair, Raven Boy,' said the girl.

'So what's your name, then?'

'I won't tell you.'

'Why not?'

'I have several reasons,' she said,

standing up and bumping her head on the tree trunk. 'Ow! First, because you won't tell me yours, but mostly because it's really silly and I'm really embarrassed about it.'

'Are you?' said Raven Boy. That was something to think about. Someone else who was embarrassed about their name. 'Well, tell me what it begins with.'

'Why?'

'So I can guess it.'

'E. But you'll never guess.'

'Elf.'

'No!' said the girl, 'that would be stupid.'

'Why? You look like an elf. Like an elf girl. Ha! Elf Girl!'

'I do not!'

'Yes, you do. You have blonde hair and you have pointy ears and you're tiny. Elf Girl.'

That seemed to make her very cross and she stamped on Raven Boy's foot.

'I AM not TINY!' she roared, in a tiny voice.

'No, you're just short for your height. I understand. Elf Girl.'

9

'Huh. Raven Boy.'

'Elf Girl.'

'Raven Boy.'

'Elf Girl.'

This went on for some time.

Then Elf Girl gasped.

'Oh!' she cried. 'We've been here all night. We must have been knocked out. I remember trees falling, and seeing silver stars whizzing around inside my head! We have to get out! I have to see if my family is safe!'

'You're right. I shall summon the badgers to help us.'

Elf Girl snorted.

'You'll do what?'

'I'll summon the badgers . . .'

'Yes, I heard you the first time. Are you trying to tell me you can talk to animals? That's not possible. You can't do it.'

'I can! Well, not exactly, but I can communicate with them. I'll just see if they're around and can dig us out . . . Hey! Badgers!'

Elf Girl watched him for a moment, her mouth slowly dropping open.

'Good luck with that, Raving

10

Boy. I'm going to start digging.'

And she did, but she'd only been digging for a few moments, when the black and white stripy snout of a badger suddenly pushed through the earth.

Elf Girl jumped with surprise and hit her head on the tree trunk again.

'Ow!'

Raven Boy noticed that the tips of her ears were going red, and her eyebrows were making funny shapes, and he guessed she might be cross again. But minutes later and there was a big hole, big enough to climb out through.

Elf Girl shook her head, picking soil from underneath her fingernails.

Raven Boy patted the badger.

'Good badger,' he said.

TWO

Elf Girl's mother has a magic bow that she's been promising to give to her daughter for ages. But you know what mums are like.

'Okay, Raven Boy, I'm impressed,' said Elf Girl. 'Wow, in fact. But I've got to

13

run. Goodbye.'

She turned to go.

'Wait!' said Raven Boy. 'Where are you going?'

'I'm going to find my family. We all have our own huts. My mum and dad. My aunts and uncles. They may be flat for all I know.'

'I'm coming with you.'

'Are you? Why?'

Raven Boy looked around. He pointed at the tree.

'That was my home. I don't have anywhere to sleep now.'

'Your home? The top of a tree? You're weirder than I thought.'

'Why's it weird? It's safe in the treetops.'

'So choose another tree.'

'I liked that one,' said Raven Boy, picking a feather out of his coat and sticking it behind his ear. 'It's not that simple. And anyway, this is a dangerous forest, you know. All sorts of scary things are lurking in it. It's safer up there than on the ground, as

long as you're in the right tree. Well, it was until last night.'

Elf Girl started to walk, and Raven Boy walked alongside her.

'What do you think it was, anyway? That made the trees fall down. It wasn't windy at all last night.'

'I don't know . . .' said Elf Girl. 'Had you been living in that tree for a long time?'

'A few weeks. After a while I get bored of the view and move to a new treetop. Why?'

'So you were living up there above my head and I never knew it.'

'I don't come down very often. Like I said, it's . . .'

'. . . dangerous down here. You might think so, but I don't.'

'Maybe it isn't if you're like you.'

Elf Girl glared at him. The tips of her ears began to get red again.

'Like me . . .?'

'Yes, you know. Tiny and . . .'

She stamped on his foot again.

'Ow. Please stop doing that. I just meant you can probably hide. Be invisible, almost.'

'I guess that's true,' said Elf Girl. She stopped and pointed. 'We need to go that way.'

'What's that mark?' asked Raven Boy, squinting at her arm.

Elf Girl covered her arm with her hand but Raven Boy had seen the mark on the inside of her left forearm.

'My, you're a nosy bird, aren't you?' she said, snappily. 'I don't know. It's some kind of birthmark. I've always had it.'

'But it's more like a scar. And it's the shape of an arrow. A perfect arrow shape. It's like a magic elf mark. You are an elf! You are!'

Elf Girl looked at the mark.

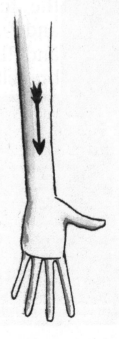

'Magic?' she muttered. 'Don't talk to me about magic. Come on! It's not far now.'

They walked through the forest. The sun shone and tiny birds tweeted and flitted from branch to branch.

'So what does your name begin with, then? Your real one?'

Raven Boy peered at her closely with his almost black eyes.

'R. But you'll never guess.'

'And it's not Raven?'

'Hardly.'

'Rupert.'

'Uh-uh.'

'Roger.'

'Nope.'

'Ricky.'

'Not even close.'

'Rudolph.'

'I'd be proud of *that*. No.'

'Wow!'

'That doesn't begin with R,' said Raven Boy, and then realised that Elf Girl was not playing that game anymore.

'Oh no!' she wailed. 'Look!'

Ahead of them were more toppled

trees. Whole chunks of the forest were missing, and underneath the trees, Raven Boy could see the remains of a couple of small huts.

'Is that where your mother and father . . .?'

Elf Girl nodded. Her lip trembled.

'If they are flat,' she said. 'I shall be very cross indeed.'

Raven Boy touched her arm.

'I'll go and look,' he said. 'You wait here.'

He was back again in no time.

'I can't see anyone. They must have all run away, like we did.'

'But where did they go?'

'Probably to look for you. I found this. What is it?'

Raven Boy held up a stick. A very fancy stick. It was smooth and curved and slightly thinner at each end.

'Oh!' cried Elf Girl. 'It's my mum's bow. It's been in our family forever. She wouldn't have left without that. Not unless they were running for their lives . . .'

21

'Bow?' asked Raven Boy. 'If you don't mind me saying, it's probably not a very good bow. It doesn't have a string on it.'

'It's a magic bow, stupid. It doesn't need a string.'

'A magic bow? Oh this'll be good! Go on, show me some magic then.'

Elf Girl glared, snatched the bow from Raven Boy, and slung it over her shoulder, crossways.

'It is a magic bow and I don't have time to show you now. I'm going to go back to my hut, in case they've gone there to look for me.'

Elf Girl looked very worried. So worried that Raven Boy felt rather sorry for her.

'Come on,' he said. 'Let's hurry. We might have missed them in the trees.'

'What's left of them,' Elf Girl said. 'Why has the forest fallen down?'

Raven Boy shook his head, quickly, in a curiously bird-like way.

'I don't know,' he said, thoughtfully, 'But I have a nasty feeling that something bad is happening. Hundreds of trees falling in one night doesn't make sense. It's as if a giant hand has pulled them up! But that's crazy.'

They reached the remains of Elf Girl's hut.

'So why do you live away from the others?' Raven Boy asked.

'We all live in our own huts. It's easier to hide than if you're in one big group that anyone could see.'

'But if they came here and found your hut like that,' said Raven Boy, pointing at the massive tree trunk, 'they probably think you're . . . you know . . . squashed.'

'Look!' cried Elf Girl. 'There's a note.'

She grabbed the note.

But not fast enough.

'Is that your name?' Raven Boy

laughed.

'Say it out loud and I'll kill you.'

Raven Boy stepped back.

Elf Girl gave him another glare and then read the note. Her eyebrows knotted.

'They were here!' she said. 'They think I've run away.'

'You had.'

'They say that everyone's huts are wrecked and they've gone to hide. But they'll come back tomorrow to see if I'm here, and every day after that.'

'That's good!'

'So all we need to do is wait . . .'

'Fine. What shall we do in the meantime?'

'Richard?'

'That again? Nope.'

'Rumpelstiltskin?'

'Are you trying to make me laugh . . .?'

They sat down, and waited, and neither of them noticed that they were sitting in a hole in the ground. A wide, deep hole, shaped, funnily enough, like an enormous foot.

THREE

Raven Boy has always been able to speak to animals, he can't remember when he learned. Or how.

'So where are your family, anyway?' asked Elf Girl. They'd been waiting a long time and the sun beams were spreading lazily across the leaves of the forest floor.

'I don't have one,' said Raven Boy.

'You must have.'

'Why must I?'

Elf Girl couldn't answer that.

'So you live alone. In the trees? What do you do?'

'What do you mean, what do I do? I eat, I sleep, I find food, I eat again. I count how many annoying girls I meet. That kind of thing. What do you do that's so amazing?'

Elf Girl couldn't answer that either.

It got dark, and still Elf Girl's mum and dad had not re-appeared.

'Maybe we should go and look for them instead,' suggested Raven Boy.

'Yes, but, the thing with that is, they've gone to hide.'

'So?'

'So we're very good at hiding. If we don't want to be seen, it's very hard to see us.'

'Really?'

'Yes, really. See that tree over there …?'

Elf Girl pointed and Raven Boy looked.

The tree was, to be honest, pretty boring, apart from the fact that it was still standing while many others were not.

When he looked back, Elf Girl had vanished.

'Whoah!' he cried. 'Where'd you go?'

'Here,' said Elf Girl, moving out of some tall grass nearby.

'I take your point.'

'So, what do we do now?'

'We wait.'

They waited some more, and then it got dark. Really dark. No moon to be seen, no stars in the sky. A thin bank of cloud had rolled in and blotted them out, and down on the forest floor Raven Boy's nose twitched nervously.

'You know,' he said. 'I'd be much happier if we did our waiting at the top of a tree.'

'There's no way I'm climbing up a tree. In the dark.'

'I'm just saying. It's not safe down here.'

29

'It's not safe up there, either. You want to fall off another one of those things?'

Raven Boy sulked for a bit.

'So how long do we wait?'

'You don't have to wait at all.'

'I thought you might want me to,' said Raven Boy.

Elf Girl shrugged.

'Suit yourself.'

Three days later, there was no sign of Elf Girl's parents.

'They're not coming,' said Raven Boy.

Elf Girl stamped on his foot.

'You might be right,' she said. 'Something must have happened to them. I have to go and look for them.'

'I thought you said they'd be

30

impossible to find?'

'I have to try. I can't just sit about here doing nothing for the rest of my life. With trees falling down all around me. I mean, anything could happen to us. Anything could happen to them! We have to do something. I have to . . . Raven Boy, are you listening to me?'

She stopped.

Raven Boy was staring up into the trees, whispering.

'Are you feeling all right? Oi! Raven Boy!'

Raven Boy looked round, and he looked worried.

'I was talking to the birds.'

'Not that again . . .'

'Hey, remember the thing with the badgers?'

Elf Girl held up a tiny elfish hand.

'Yes, I remember the thing with the badgers. So, what do the little birdies have to say?'

'They say we should run.'

'Run? Why?'

'They didn't say, they . . . Oh. I think that's why.'

Raven Boy stared behind Elf Girl, who turned to see another tree crashing towards them.

'Run!' they both yelled, and after last time, they were smart enough to run to the side. Unfortunately, they ran into each other, and were only just in time to pick themselves up before the tree smashed down, right where they'd been standing.

After the noise of the tree falling had died away, they could hear another sound. Thump, thump, thump, thump, and with each thump, the ground shook.

Something was coming. Something big, and from the way Raven Boy's nose twitched, something smelly.

They caught a glimpse of something enormous, and as Raven Boy cried

'Eep!', Elf Girl dragged him by the scruff of the neck into a bush.

'Wowsers,' whispered Elf Girl.

Raven Boy fainted.

There, standing by the tree it had just uprooted, was an ogre. Nearly as tall as the trees themselves, it stank to high heaven, and half way back. Its face was uglier than a toad's bottom, its teeth could have chewed a dragon in half, and its enormous eyes were scouring the forest.

Far below it, the bush quivered.

Raven Boy came round, saw the ogre, and fainted again.

Elf Girl shook him awake.

'Look!' she whispered, as the ogre thumped over to another tree, and with a mighty shove, sent it crashing down, just like the others.

'Eep,'

cheeped Raven Boy.

The ogre turned and looked right at their bush.

The bush shivered. Inside it, Raven Boy was trying to act out that Elf Girl should use her magic bow. Elf Girl was trying to explain without words that she didn't think it was a good idea. But Raven Boy was being persistent, so she began to point the bow as though she was going to draw back on it, even though it didn't have a string.

The bush shook some more, but the ogre seemed not to notice, as it stomped off to find another tree to push over.

Raven Boy stood up.

'Look! Look at the forest! It's going to destroy it all!'

'If it goes on like this, there'll be nothing left! And then what will happen to all the little creatures?'

'And the Elf Girls?'

'And the Raven Boys?'

Raven Boy and Elf Girl looked at each other, very seriously.

'We have to do something!' cried Elf

Girl.

'But what? How can we stop that thing? And why is it doing it anyway?'

'And where are my parents?'

'And what are we going to do?'

'You said that already,' said Elf Girl. 'But yes, what are we going to do . . .? Unless . . .'

'Unless what?'

'Unless, I've thought of something which might help us but which I'm too scared to even think about so I'm not going to say it to you in case you say it's what we really have to do and then we really have to do it, which I don't want to do because it's really scary.'

'Which is . . .?'

'You think I'm going to tell you, just like that?'

'If it's our only hope, then yes. I do.'

'It is our only hope,' said Elf Girl, sighing.

She stamped on Raven Boy's foot.

'Ow! What was that for?'

'Well, I'm cross, and I can't very well stamp on my own foot, can I?'

'Come on, then. You have to tell me. What's our only hope?'

'It's this. There are three things we need to know.'

She counted on her fingers.

'One, what is this ogre up to? Two, how can we stop it? Three, and most importantly, where have my parents got to?'

'So?'

'We need answers to three impossibly hard questions, and there's only one place to go for answers to questions like that.'

'Which is?'

'I'm coming to that. Only I wish I wasn't because it's the scary part. They say that, deep in the dark woods, in the oldest part of the forest, lives a woman who knows the answer to anything. And everything.'

'What's so scary about that?' asked Raven Boy. 'Let's get going!'

'Hah!' cried Elf Girl. 'Not so fast! There's something I haven't told you yet. This woman is a witch! That's why they call her the Witch Who Knows Everything. And her hut is guarded by a terrifying beast. Only if you defeat the beast is she prepared to answer your questions . . . And she's not the only scary thing that lives there. There are so many dangers, it's called Fright Forest.'

Raven Boy was very quiet.

'Meep,' he said. He blinked.

'But we have to do it!' cried Elf Girl.

'Are you sure we couldn't just run away again?'

'No! Yes, I mean yes, I'm sure. We have to go and find the Witch Who Knows Everything! And quickly! Before there's no forest left and while my parents are still in one piece. There's just one problem.'

'Which is?'

'I don't know which way it is to the oldest part of the forest.'

'Well, aren't you glad you met me?'

asked Raven Boy, 'Because I can find out.'

'Don't tell me,' said Elf Girl rolling her eyes, 'You're going to ask the little animals?'

Raven Boy nodded.

'Yes, I'm going to ask the little animals. And you should stop being so rude.'

Elf Girl looked sheepish. Raven Boy was right; she did need his help, after all.

FOUR

The forest where Raven Boy lives
is huge, but he's not scared of it.
Unlike Fright Forest . . .

'So why didn't you use the bow?' Raven
Boy asked as they walked off through
the forest.

43

Elf Girl kept walking.

'Well? Why didn't you use it?'

'So. How do you know where we're going?' Elf Girl replied, which wasn't a reply at all, and which Raven Boy did not fail to notice.

'I asked the deer,' he said.

'The deer, this time?' asked Elf Girl, raising her eyebrows.

'Yes, the deer,' Raven Boy said. 'I asked them where the heart of the forest is, and they say it's north, about three days' walk. I asked if they knew of the Witch Who Knows Everything, and they said we should give up now and run away.'

'Did they actually say that?'

'Well . . . not exactly. But that's what I felt when I talked to them.'

'Felt? You felt?'

Elf Girl rolled her eyes. The tips of her pointy ears quivered.

'You couldn't ask one of your little forest friends if there's a nice tavern around here somewhere, could you? I'm starving.'

'I already have.'

Elf Girl rolled her eyes even harder.

44

Raven Boy ignored her.

'There's an old inn at the head of the river. We should be there by nightfall.'

'I hope so,' said Elf Girl. 'I don't like this bit of the forest. It seems less friendly than where we live, somehow.'

It was true.

The trees seemed to peer in at them from all sides, and it was darker and more tangled here. Now, when

something rustled in the undergrowth, they would jump at the sound, startled. Cobwebs stroked their faces as they ducked under low branches, and thorns snagged at Raven Boy's long black coat tails, making him think someone was grabbing him.

'That ogre hasn't been pushing trees down around here then,' Raven Boy said.

'Nope, but I have the feeling this is the sort of wood where you find robbers and rascals and really bad people like that.'

Raven Boy nodded. He looked at Elf Girl's bow again.

'So, why didn't you use it? It might be helpful to have a little protection in Fright Forest. You do know how to use it, don't you?'

Elf Girl was silent in the gathering gloom.

'Aha! That's it! You don't know how to use it.'

'I do!' protested Elf Girl. 'It's just that it can be a little . . . unpredictable.'

'Unpredictable?   What's   that supposed to mean?'

'Whether it works or not. And when. And how. And . . .'

'Let's just hope we don't meet any rascally robbers then,' said Raven Boy.

They walked for ages and by the time they found the tavern the first stars had started to twinkle in the velvety black night sky. Raven Boy and Elf Girl were hungry. Ravenous in fact.

The tavern was called At The Sign of the Plump Piglet, which, as Raven Boy said, looked as if it would save their bacon. It seemed very inviting after their long day tramping through the forest.

The tavern was full.

They sat at a table and a woman, who they took to be the landlady, came over.

'Yes?' she said. She didn't seem very friendly, and glared at them, which was odd because she seemed to be able to look in two directions at once. Which in fact she could, since she was cross-eyed.

'Ah, yes, hello,' said Raven Boy. 'We'd very much like something to eat, please. And a nice mug of bark-beer, or whatnot?'

The landlady peered down at him. And at Elf Girl, though she was sitting on the other side of the table.

'Or whatnot? You'd like some whatnot, would you?'

'Yes, but mostly just some food. Please.'

'And you have money to pay for this, do you?'

'Ah,' said Raven Boy, and looked at Elf Girl. 'I don't, but she does.'

Elf Girl snorted.

'Me? I don't have any money.'

'No money, no food,' snapped the landlady.

'Well,' said Raven Boy, brightly. 'What do you have that's free?'

A few moments later they found themselves sitting on their backsides outside the door of the tavern.

'Nuts,' sighed Elf Girl. 'You might have said you don't have any money.'

'So might you. And why would I have money anyway?'

'What do you mean? Are you saying you live without any?'

'Pretty much.'

'But how do you buy food?'

Raven Boy tilted his chin up, stuck his nose out, striking a noble pose.

'The forest sustains me.'

'That's lovely, but what do you actually eat?'

'Anything I can get. The birds have taught me which berries to eat, for example. I probably eat what you do.

You live in the forest too.'

'Yes, but we go shopping in the village every now and again too. Are you trying to tell me you eat nuts and squirrels?'

'Yes, but not so many squirrels. I feel bad about that. You know, when you can talk to them, it rather changes things.'

Elf Girl blinked a couple of times.

'I can imagine . . . So, now what? I shall have to eat *you* if we don't get a better offer soon.'

At that exact moment, three men came out of the inn. They looked rather funny because there was a big one, a middle-sized one, and a small one, as if they came in a set.

The small one came over. He was ugly looking, but he smiled at them.

'Hello friends,' he said.

'Er, hello,' said Elf Girl.

'We couldn't help but see the awful way you were treated in there. No money, eh? Nothing to eat? Night-time coming on. We sympathise, don't we?'

He turned to the other two, who took a moment before nodding and saying 'yep' a lot.

'So we thought the least we could do is invite you back to our house for some soup and bread and bark-beer. Would that be nice?'

Raven Boy's eyes nearly fell out of his head.

'Really?' he asked eagerly. 'Food?'

'And whatnot.'

'Yes, please,' said Raven Boy.

Elf Girl nudged him.

'Are you sure it's a good idea?' she whispered, but she was feeling very hungry herself, so when Raven Boy said 'yes' and 'what can possibly go wrong?'

she went along eagerly too, through the
woods to the three men's house.

FIVE

Elf Girl loves shoes, especially her cool, pointy boots. They pinch her toes, but it's worth it for the look.

'You wouldn't believe what we saw this morning,' Raven Boy was saying to the three men as they fussed and fretted

55

about which pot to make the soup in. It was dusk outside and Raven Boy and Elf Girl were unbelievably hungry by now.

'This enormous ogre pushing trees down! Destroying the forest! There won't be any of it left if he goes on. We have to stop him.'

'And find my family,' said Elf Girl. 'My, my,' she added, 'that's a simply enormous pot you've got there. I'm not sure we're *that* hungry. That would be an awful lot of soup.'

The tallest of the three men turned round.

'Heh,' he said.

The small one bustled over to them.

'Now you just sit back while we get the cooking going. Sit down, take it easy. You must be tired.

We won't need you yet.'

'Need us?'

'For eating,' said the little man. 'For eating our soup that we are about to make you. How about some bark-beer? Or whatnot?'

He held out a couple of mugs.

'Ooh, yes please,' said Raven Boy. 'Running away from ogres is thirsty work.'

'Raven Boy,' said Elf Girl, suddenly feeling that maybe something was not quite right. 'Are you sure you ought to drink that?

'Shh,' said Raven Boy. 'I know what I'm doing.'

He took a swig from the mug, and grinned.

'Delicious,' he declared.

Elf Girl shrugged and took a sip.

She frowned, then she smiled.

'Delightful!'

Then they both fell into a deep sleep on the floor.

'Drugged,' said the little man. 'Right boys, get their clothes off and get them in that pot. I'm famished. Then let's go and pick some vegetables.'

'Do I have to have vegetables?' asked the big one.

'Yes,' said the small one, 'you have to have vegetables or your teeth will fall out.'

When Elf Girl and Raven Boy woke up again their toes felt rather hot. And in fact most of them felt rather hot, as they were tied up and sitting in a large cauldron over the fire.

'Eep!' wailed Raven Boy. 'They're cooking us.'

'Never mind that!' wailed Elf Girl. 'We've got no clothes on. Don't look!'

'So we haven't,' said Raven Boy, looking. 'Well, well. I guess it's just like being in a bath. There's nothing wrong with that. I have one every year if I can manage it.'

'Raven Boy, you are being particularly dumb. It may feel like a bath at the moment, but very soon we are going to feel like boiled potatoes.'

'Eep.'

'Yes, eep. And this is all your fault so what are you going to do about it?'

'Why is it my fault?'

'"Let's just drink bark-beer with these three strange men we've never met before . . ." That good enough for you?'

'Well, let's think. For a start,

they don't seem to be around at the moment, so let's get out of here.'

'I would agree with you, if I could see any way of getting out of this pot.'

'Aha! But that's why you ought to trust me more.'

'Really? Why's that?'

'Because I will summon one of my

animal friends to help us.'

'Oh please. What animal friends? We're in some cannibals' hovel. Who are you going to summon? A woodlouse? A determined beetle? A really big spider?'

'Uh-uh,' said Raven Boy. 'Him . . .'

He nodded at the shelf above the pot, where a sniffy little rat was, well, sniffing about.

'Of course, if you don't believe me, I can always get him to only chew through my ropes . . .?'

'Oh, no, no, no . . .' said Elf Girl. 'Please! And tell him to be quick. They might come back at any second.'

'Come on, Rat, if you'd be so good.'

Within a few moments the sniffy little rat was chewing through their ropes and they were climbing out of the pot.

'Look!' cried Elf Girl. 'Our clothes! Thank goodness.'

'Grab them and let's run. The back door's open! Hurry!'

They hopped out of the door in a

higgledy-piggledy kind of way, because running and trying to get dressed at the same time is difficult.

They flumped down in the dewy moss under a big oak, and as they did, there was a sudden scuttling in the grass.

It was the sniffy little rat.

He squeaked at them.

'What does that mean?' asked Elf Girl.

'It means, he's hungry.'

'That makes three of us,' said Elf Girl.

'At least we're alive,' said Raven Boy.

'Yes, thanks to you. And this little chap.'

The rat squeaked.

'What does that mean?' Elf Girl asked.

Raven Boy raised an eyebrow.

'He's still hungry.'

'Never mind that now. We need to find somewhere to spend the night.'

'I don't suppose I could convince you to try a treetop, could I? For one night. I promise it will be safe.'

Elf Girl looked worried, but she nodded.

'Okay, but you have to help me climb. And maybe halfway up would be high enough.'

Raven Boy smiled.

'Halfway. No higher. Come on then.'

They climbed into the tree, which Elf Girl made hard work of in her long dress and pointy boots, but soon they found a cosy nook for her to sleep in.

They slept, until, at some point in the middle of the night, Elf Girl, who had been dreaming about trolls for some reason, woke with a shriek.

'Oh! We forgot my mum's magic bow!'

SIX

Raven Boy's favourite tree is a tall pine that scrapes the sky. He likes to sit in the top and watch the birds flying.

'We have to go back for it!' she said, for the fifteenth time, and for the fifteenth time, Raven Boy shook his head.

'No way! And get eaten again! No way!'

Elf Girl reminded him that they hadn't actually been eaten the first time.

'It's been in my family for years. If I lose it, I'll be in big trouble.'

'But it doesn't even work! It's a stick!'

'You haven't seen it work yet, that's all. And if you won't come back with me, I'll go on my own.'

'No. Absolutely not. No one's going anywhere. And that's final.'

About half an hour later, Raven Boy and Elf Girl had found their way back, with the rat scampering along beside them.

There was a light on inside the house, and raised voices, and when they peered in, they were interested

to see that the three men they'd met earlier weren't there.

Instead, there were three trolls. There was a big one, a middle-sized one, and a small one. They had faces like the insides of pigs, and they were hairier than a barber's floor.

'Eeeep!' squawked Raven Boy, dropping beneath the window like a sack of nuts.

'Trolls!' squealed Elf Girl. 'They've eaten the three men! Well, good riddance to them!'

'No, you nimwit, they *are* the men,'

hissed Raven Boy. 'It's dark now, so they're in their true form. Didn't you see—a big one, a middle-sized one, and a small one? Trolls! Well, that settles it. We're off.'

'No!' cried Elf Girl, slightly too loudly. The voices inside stopped, and they heard lumbering footsteps. Raven Boy clamped his hand over Elf Girl's mouth, and they sat underneath the window, terrified, while something sniffed the air above them.

'If I didn't know better,' said the voice of the little troll, 'I'd say there's people about . . .'

'You're just still angry because our dinner ran away,' said one of the others.

'Yeah, I am angry. And if you'd tied the knots properly, it wouldn't 'ave.'

'I did tie 'em! They was chewed through. You saw that!'

'All I saw was you being stupid again.'

'Never mind that, it's all the dinner's fault. I say we stop arguing and go and find them!'

'Yeah!'

'Yeah! And then we eat them twice. Right?'

'Right!'

'Eep,' whispered Raven Boy. 'Still want to get your bow back?'

Elf Girl glared at him.

'Yes,' she said, firmly. 'I have a plan. I'm going to cause a distraction while you go and get the bow. Right?'

'Wrong! No! Wait!'

She didn't.

Elf Girl set off around to the front of the troll's house and began shouting and calling them all sorts of names.

'Hey, Trollface! How'd you get to be so ugly? And, oh, you stink too!'

That kind of thing.

Seconds later, three hopping-mad trolls burst out of the hovel and roared at Elf Girl, whose hair suddenly curled

in fright.

'Get her, lads!' screeched the little troll, and they bowled towards her.

Elf Girl screamed as she raced off into the trees, and though she tried not to look back, she couldn't help it. It seemed trolls could run faster than she thought . . .

Raven Boy stood up. He looked at the rat.

'That's the last we'll ever see of her. Come on, we may as well see if there's any food in there, and get out of here. Normal food, I mean. A carrot for example.'

Raven Boy picked up the rat who ran up his sleeve and jumped onto his shoulder, and cautiously they sneaked to the back door and into the house.

Raven Boy began hunting through cupboards for things to eat.

'Surely even trolls like chocolate biscuits,' he was saying, when the rat began to squeak energetically.

Raven Boy looked round to see the rodent scratching at a stone pot above the fireplace.

'Something important?'

Raven Boy went over and lifted the lid. It was full of coins, silver, and some gold.

'As Elf Girl would say: wow,' said Raven Boy. 'I think we might just have to help ourselves to one or two of those.'

The rat began to squeak again.

71

'Yes!' cried Raven Boy, pocketing a handful of coins. 'I hear them too! They're coming back. Quick, out!'

They ran, and as they ducked through the door, Raven Boy snatched up Elf Girl's mum's magic bow, which was leaning against the wall.

Running a short way into the trees, Raven Boy's eyes widened as he saw that the largest of the three trolls was carrying one tiny Elf Girl over his shoulder. The other two followed, looking as angry as they were hungry. And that was pretty angry.

'Oh no!' he cried.

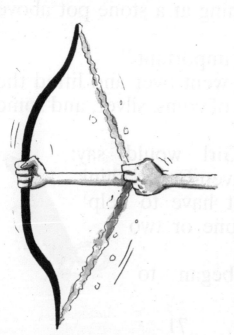

Fearlessly leaping into the open, Raven Boy waved the bow at the trolls, and made to shoot it.

'Let go of her!' he squawked. Then, 'How

does this work?'

'It won't work for you!' wailed Elf Girl from the horrible hairy back of the troll. 'Throw it to me!'

So that's what he did. Elf Girl caught the bow, where she hung from the large troll's back. He began to whirl around, trying to scrabble behind his head to grab the bow without letting go of her.

Elf Girl drew the bow, which began to shimmer, ever so slightly. It seemed as if an invisible string had appeared on it and begun to glow.

She let the glowing string go, aiming at the other two trolls.

Raven Boy jumped up and down in delight, imagining the trolls would be incinerated in moments, but then his jaw dropped.

It seemed that Elf Girl had just fired two hundred butterflies from the bow, which were fluttering happily around the ears of the trolls.

'Ooh,' said the little troll. 'You scare me.'

The middle-sized troll started to head towards Raven Boy.

'Nuts,' said Elf Girl, and she tried again.

'Hurry!' cried Raven Boy.

Elf Girl fired a second time. The bow glowed a slightly different colour, but this time, as the invisible string twanged, she fired a dozen daffodils at the little troll.

'Oh stop it,' he said, sarcastically. 'You'll set off my hay fever.'

'Elf Girl!' shouted Raven Boy, as the middle-sized troll grabbed him.

The large troll whirled, Elf Girl fired again, and this time produced a swarm of bees.

'Oh no!' wailed Raven Boy.

But the bees knew what they were doing, and there were lots of them. Thousands in fact, and they began to attack the little troll, and his two larger friends, who soon dumped Elf Girl and Raven Boy, and ran off into the trees, crying like small girls.

'Elf Girl!' shouted Raven Boy. 'You did it! Sort of! You sort of did it!'

Elf Girl beamed.

'Yes, I did, didn't I? Sort of . . .'

'Come on,' said Raven Boy, 'I think we ought to get away from here for good, in case they come back again.'

So the three of them headed into the night forest once more, until they were too tired to walk any further, and slept soundly all night on the moss under an oak tree by a babbling stream. And by morning Elf Girl's hair was nice and straight again.

SEVEN

Raven Boy doesn't know when his birthday is and is looking forward to having a really big party one day to make up for all the ones he's missed . . .

It was a beautiful morning, sunny and

warm even in that part of the forest, and small birds cheeped merrily to each other in the treetops.

Raven Boy had a happy smile on his face and was dreaming about baby blackbirds, which was all fine until he felt something nibbling his nose.

He opened his eyes to see the sniffy little rat.

'You!'

He'd quite forgotten everything. He had been deeply asleep and the baby blackbirds in his dream had been ever so cute. And then it all came back to him; the trees falling, the ogre, the trolls.

'Oh,' he said.

Then, 'Where's pointy ears?'

The rat squeaked.

'I don't mean you,' said Raven Boy. 'Maybe you need a name. Let me think. Erm. How about . . . Rat?'

Rat squeaked.

'That's settled then,' said Raven Boy. 'We ought to tell Elf Girl, but where is she?'

He stretched and looked around. There was no sign of Elf Girl anywhere.

Rat squeaked.

'I know,' said Raven Boy, 'but I don't really want to shout. You don't know who might be listening. I'll climb a tree and have a look around.'

He climbed to the top of the oak tree which they'd been sleeping under and moments later, due to his amazing tree-climbing abilities, he was in the highest branches, swaying gently in a soft breeze.

Scanning the ground below, he saw Elf Girl, not far off along the bank of the stream. Something else caught his attention then.

In the far distance, back the way they'd come, he saw yawning gaps in the forest, and, even as he watched, another tree glided slowly to its doom.

'That naughty ogre!' he cried. 'We have to hurry!'

He scrambled down from the tree at the double and ran along the bank towards Elf Girl, Rat at his side, going full pelt to keep up.

'Elf Girl! I saw another tree going down! We have to hurry.'

Elf Girl didn't turn round.

She waved a hand at Raven Boy.

'Go away,' she said.

Raven Boy stopped in his tracks.

'Go away.'

She sounded serious, really serious.

'Why? What's wrong?'

When Elf Girl didn't reply, Raven Boy grabbed her shoulder and spun her round.

'It's rude to . . .'

He stopped what he was saying.

'Oh.'

Elf Girl was crying.

'What's the matter?' asked Raven Boy.

He couldn't understand her reply. It sounded like 'mmmah-waaah-mah-paaraa-aaaa!'

He stood watching her for a bit, not knowing what to do.

'Waaa-aaaa-haah-a-mmmaah-paaraa-aaa-laa!'

'There, there,' he said, feeling awkward. 'Try and breathe. Breathing's good! It's fun sometimes! Why don't you try a little

81

bit and tell me what's wrong?'

Elf Girl looked at him for a moment, then burst into tears, her shoulders shuddering.

Raven Boy put his hand out again, and nervously gave her a gentle pat on the shoulder. Rat squeaked and jumped straight from the ground onto Elf Girl's head.

'Ow!' wailed Elf Girl, but before she could swipe Rat off, he'd disappeared down the back of her neck.

'Ow! Eee! Get out! Get off!' she screeched, and began to wriggle about as though she was dancing out of control.

As Raven Boy watched helplessly, her squeals and wails continued, and then, just as suddenly, she was giggling.

'Ow!' she screeched again, but she had a smile on her face. 'That tickles! Stop it!'

She was laughing now and Raven Boy was too.

Elf Girl was laughing so much she

fell on the ground.

She stopped giggling, and looked serious again.

'Oh!'

'Oh!' cried Raven Boy. 'Rat! You've squished Rat!'

Elf Girl looked worried, and then Rat poked his head out of the neck of her dress, and squeaked.

And that made them all laugh even more.

When they had finished, Raven Boy smiled at Elf Girl.

'What was wrong?' he asked. 'Why were you crying?'

'My parents,' she said, simply. 'I think something awful must have happened to them. And I don't know where they are.'

Raven Boy stood up.

'No, we don't. But we're going to find out.'

He looked determined, and that made Elf Girl feel better.

'Do you think we can?' she asked.

'Yes, don't you?'

Elf Girl nodded, but neither of them admitted to the other that they weren't feeling as brave as they were trying to sound.

'Which way?' Elf Girl asked.

'This way,' said Raven Boy. And when he told her that a grass snake had explained they ought to walk north along the stream, she didn't even make fun of him.

'You know, you're not bad for a boy,' Elf Girl said, and for some reason Raven Boy felt very proud about that. Though he tried not to let it show.

EIGHT

Before he met Elf Girl, Raven Boy used to have tea with a barn owl every Thursday.

They walked along the bank of the stream, which had been joined by a few other streams, until it had turned into quite a big river. The sun was shining, the trees grew taller and denser on each side of the river, and Elf Girl was playing the name game.

'Rolf?'
'Nope.'
'Rick?'
'Wrong.'
'Russell.'
'Elf Girl, do we have to play this?'
'Aha!' cried Elf Girl, 'It's Russell, isn't it? Russell. That's not *that* embarrassing you know.'
'It's not Russell,' said Raven Boy. 'I'm just really bored of that game.'
'So why don't you just tell me?'
'You can't get me that way.'
'Suit yourself,' said Elf Girl, shrugging. 'But listen, who are your

parents anyway? Someone must have given you this name for you to be embarrassed about.'

Raven Boy struck another noble pose. Elf Girl was starting to realise this might be something he did a lot, but she couldn't be sure if he was serious or not.

'The trees are my parents,' he said, his chin pointing at the sky.

'That's . . . special,' said Elf Girl.

Raven Boy blinked.

'I don't know,' he said, his chin dropping. 'Ever since I can remember, there's just been me, and the trees. And the animals.'

'The animals . . .'

'The gentle forest creatures, who have guided me since I was a small thing.'

'You're not exactly tall now.'

'I'm taller than you, Elf Girl.'

'Hah! Raven Boy talks to the little animals!'

'Hah yourself! Elf Girl has pointy ears!'

And so they went on, happily teasing each other, while Rat sat on

Raven Boy's shoulder because, as he'd explained, his little feet were tired from keeping up with the big people.

In fact, they were so busy teasing each other that Elf Girl and Raven Boy didn't notice when Rat suddenly pricked up his ears, squeaked once, and disappeared.

They were a good five minutes further down the river bank before Elf Girl suddenly said, 'Where's Rat?'

They stopped dead, and looked around.

'Have you noticed,' said Raven Boy, 'how quiet it is, all of a sudden?'

Elf Girl nodded.

'What's going on?' she whispered, above the noise of the river. 'Could you ask one of your forest chums?'

'That's just it. I can't.'

'Why not?'

'There's not one around. Not one.'

'Erm, Raven Boy,' said Elf Girl.

'What?'

'Do you see what I see?'

'Which is?'

'A large pair of eyes under a large pair of ears, in the trees, over there?'

90

'The ones that look like they belong to a large and particularly hungry wolf?'

Elf Girl gulped.

'Yes,' she whispered.

'The thing to do,' said Raven Boy, 'is walk calmly away, as though we're not scared.'

'But I am. Can't you just, you know, have a word with it and ask it not to eat us?'

'Walk faster,' said Raven Boy, walking faster. 'Two things about that. First of all, I could talk to it, but basically I would only be discussing which bit of us it's going to eat first. And secondly, it's not alone.'

Elf Girl gulped for a second time.

'Raven Boy?'

'What?'

'You know this walking faster thing?'

'Yes?'

'How do you feel about running?'

Raven Boy began to run and Elf Girl screamed.

'Hey! I take it that was a yes?' she

91

panted as she caught him up.

Raven Boy nodded.

'The river! We need to cross the river!'

He was right. Behind them, a pack of thin and ravenous wolves was already pounding hard on their trail. Their tongues were lolling out and if they'd been holding signs saying 'We're going to eat you' it couldn't have been much clearer.

'It's too deep! We'll be drowned. Isn't there a bridge?'

'Not that I can see,' cried Raven Boy. 'Quick, up into the trees.'

'What! You know I hate climbing!'

'And I hate being eaten by wolves even more. Climb!'

Raven Boy shoved Elf Girl up into the lower branches of the closest tree, and scrambled after her just as a whopping set of dribbling fangs chomped thin air right behind his heels.

'Eep!' he cried. 'Climb for your

life!'

The wolves began to jump and paw at the tree trunk.

'Climb!' shouted Raven Boy again, and in the blink of an eye, they were up in the top of the branches.

'How do you make it look so easy, Raven Boy?' gasped Elf Girl, as she clambered up behind him, panting and looking hot and bothered.

He shrugged.

'I spend most of my time up here. You kind of get used to it.'

He sat bobbing up and down on a spindly branch, picking some feathers out of his hair.

'What exactly do we do now, though?' Elf Girl asked. 'And where is Rat?'

Raven Boy pointed.

'I think that answers both your questions.'

Elf Girl saw where Raven Boy was pointing, and they watched Rat, who was perching on the tip-top of a neighbouring tree. He climbed right to the end of a branch leaning out over the river, and leapt into the branches of

a tree on the far side.

'We can't do that!' squealed Elf Girl.

'It's that or spend the rest of your life here,' said Raven Boy. 'Getting thinner.'

Elf Girl frowned.

'But we can't jump that far.'

'We won't have to. We're heavier than Rat. We just have to climb to the top of the tree. Lean a bit, and let gravity do the rest.'

'No. Way.' said Elf Girl.

Two minutes later, they were clinging onto a branch that was starting to lean at a perilous angle out over the river, as the wolves snapped and howled and prowled on the bank.

'Raven Boy!' wailed Elf Girl. 'Help!'

'Nnng,' said Raven Boy, edging further along the branch, which suddenly dropped within reach of another branch on a tree on the other bank.

'Grab it!' he cried, and they did, and swung from their tree into the air, and down on the opposite bank.

'Ow!' moaned Elf Girl.

The wolves were going loopy now, tearing up and down as their lunch got away.

'Hmm,' said Raven Boy.

'What?'

'The wolves. They're not saying very

nice things about us . . .'

Rat skipped over from his tree and sat on Raven Boy's head.

He squeaked.

'Yes, Rat. It *was* a good idea of yours.'

NINE

Raven Boy usually sleeps in a different tree every couple of weeks; it stops him getting bored. After the pine tree, his favourite is an ancient oak.

Night fell, and after the excitement

with the wolves, they were exhausted.

'It would be nice to have a fire,' Elf Girl said, as they settled down in a cosy dell for the night.

'Too risky,' said Raven Boy, and Elf Girl knew he was right.

'How far do you think it is now?' asked Elf Girl. 'Have you spoken to a small fluffy creature recently?'

'Can I just say,' said Raven Boy, 'that finding the Witch Who Knows Everything was your idea. So don't give me a hard time about it.'

'Calm down!' said Elf Girl. 'I was only asking.'

'As it happens, the general feeling among my feathery friends is that we are taking way too long and we're not even at the edge of Fright Forest yet. We ought to get there some time tomorrow. That's what a small owl told me, anyway.'

'And how will we know when we get there?'

'We'll know.'

'We will?'

'We will. Apparently it's hard to mistake it.'

'That doesn't sound good.'

Raven Boy nodded.

Rat jumped onto his head and began to clean himself.

'Charming,' said Raven Boy.

Elf Girl laughed.

'He likes you,' she said, giggling.

'Sweet,' muttered Raven Boy. 'Well, we ought to get some sleep. Then on at first light.'

'Raven Boy, I'm still hungry.'

'Me too. Tomorrow I'll find us some nuts and fruit.'

'Oh good,' muttered Elf Girl. 'Nuts and fruit. What I'd really like, really, is something big and tasty and yummy and warm.'

Now it was odd that that was what Elf Girl was after, because not so far away in the trees, three hungry trolls were thinking exactly the same thing.

'I can smell 'em,' said the big one.

'Shh!' said the small one. 'You don't want to scare 'em off again, do yer?'

'I'm hungry,' grumbled the middle-sized one.

'Which is what we're doing here, isn't it? Getting our dinner back, eh?'

'Why didn't we just stay at home and eat someone else from The Plump Piglet?' said the big one.

'Because, idiot,' said the small one, 'if word ever gets out that we let our dinner run away, no one's ever going to be scared of us again. Are they? So we have to get our dinner back.'

'And then eat it?'

'Yeah, and then eat it. Three times.'

'We must be getting close,' said the middle-sized troll. 'I can smell 'em too, now. One of them smells like pretty little flowers in the meadow. Ugh! And the other one smells like honey and jam or sumfin'. Eurgh! Disgusting!'

'Shh!' hushed the small one. 'You don't want to scare 'em off, do yer?'

And so on and so on.

Raven Boy was snoring and dreaming that a rat was nibbling his ears, which was unsurprising, because that was exactly what was happening.

Elf Girl couldn't sleep. She was too scared and besides, Raven Boy kept making snuffling sounds every now and again in between the snores, which was getting deeply annoying.

She got up and decided to go for a short walk. Just a small one, in a circle around their camp, so she wouldn't get lost in the dark.

'Maybe I'll get sleepy then,' she said to herself. 'Wait here,' she added to Rat, who squeaked at her, quietly, so as not to wake Raven Boy.

'Do you understand me too?' she wondered. 'I don't understand you. Everything you say is squeak.'

Rat squeaked, and Elf Girl went for her walk.

It was peaceful for a while, as she walked, though she found herself imagining she'd heard something. She shook her head, and walked on. Finally, she started to feel tired.

'Maybe it's time for a nap, after all.'

When she got back, two things were missing.

Raven Boy and Rat.

'I told you to wait here!' she cried, to

no one in particular.

There was a squeak beside her and Rat popped his head out of a hole in the roots of a tree nearby. He hopped onto the ground and sped over to Elf Girl.

He was shaking.

'What is it?' cried Elf Girl. 'What's wrong?'

Rat shook some more and began to circle and sniff at the ground.

Elf Girl got down on her hands and knees.

'Footprints! Well, I never knew footprints could stink! Phew!'

She held her nose.

'And there's three sets. Big ones. Middle-sized ones. And small ones. Three sizes of stinky prints! Oh no! It's the trolls again! Quick, Rat! We have to find them, they've got Raven Boy!'

Rat squeaked and scampered off into the dark trees, barely giving Elf Girl enough time to grab her mum's magic bow, and set off after him.

TEN

Fright Forest is home to eighty-seven different types of poisonous toadstools. Some of them glow in the dark.

It didn't take Elf Girl and Rat long to find the trolls. They sneaked up to a

tree and peered around it, aware there were girl-and-rat-eating monsters on the other side.

The trolls hadn't gone far, only to a quiet little spot nearby, just right in their opinion for eating small children.

There was Raven Boy, dangling upside down on the end of a rope tied round his ankles and thrown over a high branch.

He was suspended over a fire, which, fortunately for him, the trolls were having the devil of a time trying to light.

'It's your stupid fault,' said the big one to the middle one. 'You got damp wood. I told you about damp wood.'

'It's not damp. You're just rubbish with matches,' said the small one to the big one. 'Give 'em to me.'

He snatched the matches, they squabbled, and the matches spilled out of the box.

'Now look what yer done!' said the little troll.

'It was your fault.'

'Why don't you pick the matches up and just get on with cooking him? I'm 'ungry.'

'I still say we find the girl first.'

'And we said we eat the boy while we got him, and then find the girl. You was outvoted.'

'Don't I get a vote?' asked Raven Boy.

'Yeah,' said the big troll. 'Don't he get a vote?'

'Because if so,' Raven Boy went on. 'I vote you don't eat me. At all. Or anyone actually. I could show you some nice recipes for things to do with vegetables.'

'Vegetables!' spat the middle-sized one. 'I ain't voting for vegetables.'

'No! No vegetables,' shouted the small one, losing his temper. 'No vegetables. No more voting. No nothing. We cook the boy and eat 'im, and then we find the girl and eat 'er too. Gottit?'

'I'm still here, you know,' said Raven Boy. 'It's not very nice talking about eating me when I'm right here.'

He spun slowly on his rope.

'Did somebody say sumfin'?' said the middle-sized troll.

'The dinner said sumfin',' said the big

one.

'I said I don't think you should eat me,' added Raven Boy.

'The food is not supposed to have an opinion!' said the little troll. 'Will you please hurry up and roast him so he doesn't talk so much.'

'We could always bop him on the head first. You know that makes them quieter.'

'Yeah, but they always seem to be chewier when we do that.'

'Chewier! You're a troll! You're not supposed to care about chewy food!'

Behind the tree, Elf Girl watched in horror, and couldn't help shuddering as the large troll picked up all the matches and struck one against the box.

Very carefully, he knelt under the revolving Raven Boy and tried to light the fire again.

'Come on now,' said the small one. 'There's a good idiot. You light the nice little fire now.'

'Do you have to?' said Raven Boy.

'Yes, he does,' snapped the small one. And then, 'Shut up, anyway. There's rules about the dinner talking, an' all. It makes it chewy.'

'Well, I think you've got a problem

then,' said Raven Boy.

The large troll straightened up.

'It went out again,' he said. 'What did the dinner say?'

'He said we got a problem,' said the middle one.

'How's that, then?'

'Well,' said Raven Boy. 'If I'm going to get chewy if I keep talking, then you ought to bop me on the head . . .'

Elf Girl held her breath.

'. . . But if you bop me on the head,' Raven Boy continued. 'I'm going to get chewy anyway. So you've got a problem. Chewy food.'

The three trolls were enormously silent for a long time.

Then, the small one piped up.

115

'Ha! No! There's a way out of it. If you just don't talk, we don't need to bop you on the head and then you won't be chewy either way.'

'True,' said Raven Boy, 'but I'm not going to stop talking. So you're a bit stuck.'

There was another long silence, and then the large one spoke.

'So? We've 'ad worse. We'll just eat you chewy . . .'

'Yeah,' said the middle-sized one. 'Three times.'

'At least,' said the small one. 'Now get that pigging fire lit, will yer?'

'Meep!' cried Raven Boy.

Elf Girl had closed her eyes, as she tried to concentrate. At the same time, she pulled her bow back to its fullest draw, and was trying to think of something magical to make it work properly.

Rat was watching her, and was

particularly interested in the way that the arrow mark on her arm was glowing faintly.

'Pleasepleaseplease,' Elf Girl was whispering under her breath, and then she let fly, while her eyes were still shut.

'Oops,' she said, her eyes wide, as she watched a bright blue bolt of light shoot from her bow. The whole wood seemed to shine in the blue light, and it was hard to see anything for a moment.

'Oh!' she cried. 'Raven Boy?'

The light disappeared to reveal three large blue blocks of ice standing around a fourth block of ice, that hung from a tree.

Inside the blocks of ice were the trolls, and, still spinning on the rope, a very surprised-looking Raven Boy.

'Oh no!' cried Elf Girl. 'Rat, I think we ought to get that fire lit as fast as we can.'

particularly interested in the
was that the arrow mark on
her arm was glowing faintly.

'Pleasepleaseplease,' Elf
Girl was whispering under
her breath, and then she let
fly, while her eyes were still
shut.

'Oops,' she said, her
eyes wide, as she watched
a bright blue bolt of light
shoot from her bow. The whole wood
seemed to shine in the blue light, and it
was hard to see anything for a moment.

'Oh!' she cried. 'Raven Boy?'

The light disappeared to reveal
three large blue blocks of ice standing
around a fourth block of ice, that hung
from a tree.

Inside the blocks of ice were the
trolls, and, still spinning on the rope, a
very surprised-looking Raven Boy.

'Oh no,' cried Elf Girl. 'Rat, I think
we ought to get that fire lit as fast as we
can.

ELEVEN

No one's seen an ogre in Raven Boy and Elf Girl's part of the forest for years. But they can cause big problems when they do show up!

It turned out that Elf Girl was much better with matches than the trolls,

119

and she soon had some nice jolly flames underneath the block of ice that contained Raven Boy.

'I hope he can breathe,' she said to Rat.

Rat squeaked, sniffed about a lot, then squeaked again.

Not long after that, the ice around Raven Boy's head began to melt, drip by drip, and then like a tap running. Elf Girl did her best to stop the water splashing onto the fire, but by the time Raven Boy's head was almost free, the fire hissed and went out.

Elf Girl pulled and poked at the last bits of ice around Raven Boy's face, and then, with a pop, his head was free.

'Now what?' he said, taking deep breaths. 'I'm very fed up of hanging upside down. All the blood is going to my head and it feels funny.'

'I don't know what to do. Perhaps I should try the bow again . . .?'

'No!' shrieked Raven Boy. 'Eep! I mean, no, er, let's see if we can think of something else. First, I need to get down from here.'

'Yes,' said Elf Girl, ' but I don't see

. . . oh.'

Raven Boy looked where she was looking, up at his toes. He saw Rat had climbed along the branch from which Raven Boy was hanging, towards the rope.

Rat gave a squeak and began to chew.

'Rat! Wait! I'll fall on my head!'

Raven Boy looked desperately at Elf Girl, but there was nothing she could do but try to grab the slippery block of ice just as Rat chewed through the last strand of rope.

She did at least manage to stop Raven Boy from landing on his head, and Rat bounded over to them, whiskers quivering, expecting thanks.

'Rat, that was a bit silly,' Elf Girl said.

Rat turned his back and sulked.

'Ow,' said Raven Boy.

Elf Girl started giggling.

'What's so funny?' asked Raven Boy, though he could guess.

'You. You look kind of stupid.'

'Hilarious. Get me out of here, will you?'

'I would,' she said, 'but how?'

'Well, we have to do something. When the sun comes up those three are going to melt too and we need to be long gone. They'll become human again I suppose, but nevertheless . . .'

Elf Girl went up to the nearest

troll. The small one. She lit a match and peered into the block of ice. His eyes were open inside the ice, and he seemed to be looking straight at her.

'Do you think they're alive?' she asked.

'I wouldn't like to find out,' Raven Boy said.

'They look nasty. And ugly.'

'Elf Girl,' Raven Boy said, 'They might be able to hear you.'

'No, don't be silly,' she said. 'In there? I don't think so.'

But after another look at the small one she decided not to say anything more.

'Anyway, we need to get going,' she said.

'You're going to have to pull me,' Raven Boy said.

'What?'

'Get the rope. It's tied round my ankles still, isn't it? So you're going to have to pull me through the woods until the sun comes up and then I can thaw out.'

'No way!' cried Elf Girl.

But she did. She just about managed to pull Raven Boy a short way from the trolls, along a mostly flat path through the trees.

Raven Boy had been complaining non-stop, and Rat was sitting on the ice, getting a free ride, though he lifted his feet in turn to let them warm up again.

'Ow! Watch it there, that's a rough bit. Ow! Careful with me! I'm precious goods. I . . . ow!'

That kind of thing. Elf Girl was getting crosser and crosser.

'Look out for that root!' cried Raven Boy. 'Ow!'

Elf Girl dropped the rope.

'That's it! You can wait for the trolls for all I care! I've had enough! You are the bossiest, fussiest, stupidest Raven Boy I have ever met!'

'Well, can I help it if the ground's rough and you're too stupid to pull me carefully? It's not exactly cosy in here you know.'

'At least you're lying down! I'm exhausted.'

'And I'm freezing to death. Slowly! I feel like a fish in a fish shop.'

'Hah!' cried Elf Girl. 'You look like one too!'

With that she kicked the lump of ice.

'Ow!' she cried, but what she hadn't realised in the dark is that they were near the top of a long, and rather steep slope.

The ice began to slide.

'Er . . .' said Raven Boy.

'Er what?' snapped Elf Girl.

'I think I'm moving.'

Elf Girl stood with her arms folded, and her nose in the air, doing her best to look furious. When she looked down again, Raven Boy wasn't where she'd left him.

'Help!' Raven Boy warbled, and now he was hurtling as fast as a greased kangaroo down what seemed to be a very steep slope indeed. 'Help!'

'Oh!' Elf Girl squealed and began to run after him, but he was picking up speed all the time.

Now Raven Boy shot like a bullet down the slope, faster and faster.

'Eeeeeeeep!' he wailed as he went, and then there was an almighty crash as he hit a tree.

The block of ice shattered into a thousand tiny ice cubes, and Raven Boy lay on the ground in a chilly daze.

Elf Girl caught up with him, followed closely by Rat.

'Oh! I'm so sorry, Raven Boy,' she sobbed. 'Are you all right? I'm so sorry!'

Raven Boy smiled.

'Well, that worked,' he said.

'I'm sorry. I didn't mean to . . .'

'No, I mean it. I'm free. Only I'm cold. I'm so frozen I can't move!'

'You'll be able to move soon, I'm

sure. When the sun comes up.'

'And when the sun comes up, those trolls will be after us again.'

'Yes, but you slid a long way. We'll have a head start. And they'll be men, not trolls. Maybe they won't want to eat us so much.'

'I think I can feel my toes again,' Raven Boy said. 'Maybe.'

'Good! Only . . .'

'Only what?'

'Only, we have to find the Witch Who Knows Everything and get some answers. Before . . .'

'Before what?'

But he already knew what Elf Girl was going to say.

'Before it's too late.'

Raven Boy nodded.

'Meep,' he said quietly. And didn't say what he was also thinking, that it might already be too late.

TWELVE

The most dangerous thing in Fright Forest is in fact a tiny green beetle. It's poisonous enough to kill a hundred warthogs.

'Raven Boy,' said Elf Girl.
  'What?' said Raven Boy, who was

trying to stretch and get some blood flowing in his veins again. Rat sat on his head, like a furry warm hat, trying to help. And help he did, though what Raven Boy could really have used was a couple of hot water bottles.

'We need to go.'

'Well,' said Raven Boy. 'As it happens I agree with you, and I haven't been wasting my time here, you know.'

He nodded at the trees, and Rat slid off his head, clinging on to Raven Boy's ear for dear life.

'I was just having a brief chat to some

130

woodpeckers,' said Raven Boy, lifting Rat back up again.

Elf Girl opened her mouth, saw the look on Raven Boy's face, and shut it again.

'Yes, woodpeckers. Nice birds, actually. Tend to repeat themselves but very polite.'

'I'm sure,' said Elf Girl, encouragingly.

'And they said we ought to follow the river till it forks. Then we take the left fork, and follow it into the swamp.'

'The swamp?' asked Elf Girl.

'Yes, the swamp.'

'That doesn't sound like fun.'

'It isn't. The woodpeckers advised us to turn around and go home.'

'Well, I would,' said Elf Girl. 'If I had a home left to go to. Or a family.'

Tears began to well up in her eyes and Raven Boy felt bad.

'But that's not what we're going to do,' he added hurriedly, 'although . . .'

'Although what?' she sniffed.

'Although the swamp isn't the worst thing. It's the witch. The Witch Who Knows Everything. According to the

woodpeckers, she's scary. Deadly. Horrible, old, smelly, did I mention scary? And she eats children.'

'Oh,' said Elf Girl in a small voice. 'Why does everyone want to eat us?'

'Food's hard to come by, I guess. Anyway, that's not the end of it,' said Raven Boy. 'Before you even get to her, you'd have to get past the monster that guards her hut.'

Elf Girl blinked.

'Yes, I know, I told you that already.'

'I know, it's just that the birds said that no one's ever managed it.'

'They did?' she asked, in an even more tiny and miserable voice.

Raven Boy nodded.

'But we're not going to give up. We're going to get the answers we need and sort out the ogre and find your family and everything's going to be all right.'

Elf Girl cheered up a little.

'And you can ask your animal friends as we go. They must know more about this monster. How we might get past it, for example.'

'Right!' said Raven Boy, but he didn't look too sure. 'And if all else fails, you can use your bow again, yes?'

Elf Girl forced a smile.

'It's worked for us, so far. Hasn't it? Sort of . . .'

So they set off again.

'I still feel like a fish,' Raven Boy grumbled.

'You smell like one too,' said Elf Girl, sniggering.

But the sniggering soon stopped, as the forest was getting thicker all the time. They had to force their way through bramble bushes, under spiky shrubs and past towering trees. Creepers hung down, tangling around their ankles like tentacles from the deepest, darkest oceans. A foul mist sprang up and once or twice they felt eyes watching them from the gloom.

Suddenly, they pulled up short.

'Look!' cried Elf Girl. 'The fork in the

133

river!'

'So, let's go and find the swamp.'

They did. Morning came, but the forest was so thick that it wasn't much lighter than in the night-time.

The morning wore on and became the afternoon, and Rat got tired of walking and sat on Raven Boy's head again. After he'd fallen off a couple of times, he tried exploring other parts of Raven Boy, and finally settled for the pocket of his coat, from which  his nose emerged from time to time, sniffing the air.

The trees around them began to change. They got shorter but closer together, and the space between them was filled with thick and vicious bushes. Then the ground underneath started to get spongy and wet. The river had petered into a trickle that twisted this way and that among the trees, trees which were now strange and gnarled, with long strands of some kind of moss hanging from them.

The sounds of the forest had changed too, bird calls were odd and unfamiliar. There were no more pleasant cheeping sounds from tiny birds, but instead, occasional loud squawks and cries that sounded like warnings to Elf Girl and Raven Boy.

Without realising it, they had stopped talking, and walked in silence, until suddenly they both spoke together.

'Which way do we go?' they said.

Elf Girl raised her eyebrows.

'Well?'

'I don't know,' Raven Boy whispered back. 'The river has disappeared. Wait. I'll see if I can find anyone to talk to. Wait here!'

Elf Girl swallowed.

'Don't go far! Don't be long! I don't like it here.'

Raven Boy nodded.

'I'll just go in a circle and see who I

can find. Rat can stay with you.'

'Well, that makes me feel a whole lot safer.'

Rat squeaked huffily as Raven Boy pulled him from his pocket and handed him to Elf Girl.

'Can you understand me?' Elf Girl asked. 'Really?'

Rat squeaked again and Elf Girl was quiet. Raven Boy had disappeared into the thickly crowded trees.

Elf Girl sat down.

'Well, Rat,' she said, 'if you can understand me, I'm going to tell you a story, just to pass the time until Raven Boy gets back, and so we don't get scared . . . I mean, bored. So we don't get bored. It's a funny story and it's called Elf Girl and Raven Boy Are Really Brave And Never Get Scared. Ready? It goes like this . . .'

Suddenly, there was a rustling noise and Elf Girl screamed.

Raven Boy stuck his head out of the bushes.

'Shh! Don't do that!'

'You scared me stupid!' Elf Girl said angrily, her ears turning pink.

136

'I didn't mean to,' Raven Boy said. 'I just couldn't find my way back. Anyway, I just had a nice chat to a turtle.'

'A turtle? Raven Boy, are you sure you can talk to animals? We might be totally lost and miles from anywhere, and all because you think you can talk to turtles.'

Raven Boy looked offended.

'I'm offended,' he said. 'Shall I tell you what the turtle said, or not?'

Elf Girl nodded, but she was still a bit angry that Raven Boy had scared her.

'She, the turtle that is, said we should turn back and go home . . .'

'But . . . !'

'But we're not going to, I know!' Raven Boy said, before she could go on. 'And she said that if we really wanted to go and be eaten (her words) by the witch and her monster, then we're nearly there. In fact, it's just past the next clump of trees.'

He stopped and Elf Girl stared at him.

'So then, are we going?' he asked.

Now Elf Girl stared at the trees.

'Over there?' she asked. 'The witch, and her, er, monster.'

Raven Boy nodded.

'We can always . . .'

'No!' cried Elf Girl. 'We're going. If it kills us.'

And she began to stomp towards the trees.

Raven Boy picked Rat up and sat him on his head.

'That's just what I'm afraid of,' he said, as they followed the small but determined girl who looked a lot like an elf into the trees.

THIRTEEN

Ogres eat anything; but whole ponies and wriggling children are their favourite foods.

The clump of trees in question sat on a rise in the ground. They got down on their hands and knees and crawled underneath the lowest branches of the trees, more of the strange twisted ones with moss. They poked their noses out and looked down into a hollow, hardly daring to breathe.

There was the witch's hut.

It looked exactly like a witch's hut should. Old, and falling to pieces, with a battered roof, and crumbling chimney stack. Outside was a veranda which had also seen better days. It had a handrail in places, but missing in others, and there were holes in the planks of the porch. Hanging from hooks in the eaves of the hut were all sorts of pots and pans, a tin bathtub, and lots of things that they didn't recognise, and didn't want to either.

'I don't see any monster,' whispered Raven Boy, very quietly.

'Can't you ask one of your . . .'

'No one about. Not a single creature. I guess they all stay away from the witch. And her little pet.'

'But where is it?' Elf Girl asked.

'Maybe it's gone for a walk. Maybe we can go right down there and . . .'

'No! Wait! Look underneath the hut!

Something's coming!'

It was true. They could see underneath the hut, which sat on blocks of wood, through to the other side. And on the other side, something was moving in the darkness. It was coming round the hut, towards the front.

Rat squeaked.

Raven Boy squeaked.

Elf Girl squeaked, and went a funny shade of green.

The monster appeared.

It made a tiny mewing sound.

It was a small white kitten.

'It's a small white kitten,' said Raven Boy.

He stood up and started towards it.

'Wait!' cried Elf Girl, pulling him back. 'Supposing it's not the monster? Supposing it's the monster's lunch? Or supposing it is the monster and it's just disguised as a kitten? Maybe it can change into other animals.'

Raven Boy shook himself free and marched down the slope.

'Hey, Kitty! Is your mummy at home? We want a word with . . .'

That was as far as he got, as suddenly the kitten leapt for him; clawing, biting, scratching, hissing . . .

Raven Boy yelled and howled.

'Noooo! Get it off! Ow! Nooooo!'

The kitten was deadly, and very soon it had Raven Boy pinned to the ground and in big trouble.

'Rat! Stay here! I have to do something!' cried Elf Girl and ran down the slope yelling. 'Get off! Get off him!'

That was enough to distract the

killer kitten, and Raven Boy slithered free and was up a tall tree faster than a jet-pack monkey. The kitten tried to follow, but couldn't quite manage it. It kept trying and Raven Boy looked down at it, scared and shocked.

Suddenly the door to the hut flew open, and a tattily dressed figure rushed towards Elf Girl.

She only had time to realise that the mess of rags and hair was the witch, before the nasty old hag bopped her on the head with a heavy stick and dragged her back into the hut, with surprising strength, leaving Raven Boy up the tree, still trapped by the small fluffy kitten. Elf Girl's bow lay on the ground where she'd fallen.

There was a scurrying sound beside him, and Raven Boy saw that Rat had joined him.

'Eep!' cried Raven Boy. 'Now what do we do?'

The kitten continued to leap and claw at the tree trunk, which, though tall, was not sturdy.

'We can't stay up here for ever, Rat,' said Raven Boy. 'And Elf Girl! The witch could have ...'

He stopped, and swallowed hard. He didn't want to think what the witch might already have done to Elf Girl. Raven Boy realised that he had started to like Elf Girl, quite a lot.

'Rat, do you think you can get away from here if I distract the kitten for five seconds?'

Rat squeaked.

'Good! Then go into the forest,

and find the biggest wolf you can. Something that can give this stroppy feline a run for its milk, yes?'

Rat squeaked again, and Raven Boy started to climb down from the tree, gingerly dangling one foot closer to the white beast.

That was enough to send the kitten into a frenzy, and it lunged, sinking all four razor-sharp claws into Raven Boy's backside.

'Eeeeeeeeeeeeep!' he wailed, but by then Rat was long gone.

FOURTEEN

**There's supposed to be a pool
of vanishing in the middle of
the forest, but no one knows for
certain, because no one's ever
come back from it.**

'Hurry, Rat!' cried Raven Boy, but he

needn't have worried. Rat was back in the flick of a whisker, and with help.

Help, however, turned out not to be a large, kitten-eating wolf, but some kind of swamp dog.

'Rat, is that a swamp dog?'

Rat squeaked.

'Rat, I hate to be mean, but I don't think...'

But as soon as the swamp dog set eyes on the kitten, it leapt at it, long sharp fangs at the ready.

A moment later, the two creatures were a tumbling ball of fur and claws and teeth, and Raven Boy was able to shimmy down the tree safely.

'Give him one from me, swamp dog,' said Raven Boy, rubbing his bottom as he hurried towards the hut. 'If I've learned one thing today,' he said, 'it's that the smaller something is, the meaner it fights.'

Wasting no more time, Raven Boy grabbed Elf Girl's bow and burst into the hut, brandishing it as if he knew what he was doing.

'Stop that right there!'

Elf Girl was hanging upside down

by her ankles from a beam in the roof
of the hut, and the witch was standing
underneath with her hands on her hips.

'What is it with you bad people?'
Raven Boy asked. 'Why do you guys
have to hang everyone upside down all
the time?'

'Who are you?' screeched the witch.

'I'm Raven Boy!' cried Raven Boy,
dramatically. 'And if you've harmed a
hair on Elf Girl's head I'll . . .'

'You'll what?' said the witch. 'And
who's Elf Girl anyway?'

'She is!' said Raven Boy, pointing.

'And she's my friend.'

Raven Boy supposed that was true. He looked at the witch for the first time. It was gloomy in the hut, and the witch had a big tatty cloak, and a hood which covered her head too. But Raven Boy had noticed something.

'Take your hood off,' he said.

'No,' said the witch.

'Take your hood off, or I'll shoot,' he said, waving the bow at her.

'With that stick? Oh, please,' said the witch.

'I mean it,' said Raven Boy, sounding as tough as he could. 'It's a magic bow.'

The witch paused for a moment, and then pulled down her hood.

'You're not a

witch!' cried Raven Boy.

The witch certainly didn't look like one. She wasn't old, she wasn't ugly, or warty. And she didn't look scary. At all.

'I *am* a witch,' said the witch.

Raven Boy thought about this.

'I don't want to be rude,' he said, 'but you really don't look like one. And the monster guarding your hut is a kitten.'

'He's a cat!' said the witch, looking insulted.

'He's a kitten. A pretty mean kitten, but he's still a kitten. You're supposed to have a big scary monster eating trespassers.'

The witch pulled her hood up, as if hiding, and then burst into tears. Her hood slipped down again.

'I know! I'm not a witch. And Tipsy is the best I could do for a guard. But I don't know what else to do!'

She sobbed some more, during which time Raven Boy stood not knowing what to do.

'Er, do you think you could let me down now?'

It was Elf Girl, who'd come round

from being bopped on the head, and seemed quite well, despite being upside down.

Raven Boy rushed over and untied her, helping her onto her feet. They looked at each other for a little while, not saying the things they were thinking.

'What's up with her?' Elf Girl said.

'She's upset because she's not a witch.'

'That's funny. I'm delighted she's not a witch. Only . . .'

'Only what?'

'Only if she's not a witch, she's not going to be able to help us. To do magic and stuff.'

At this the witch spun round.

'I can do magic!' she declared.

'So why aren't you a witch then?' asked Raven Boy.

'Because I don't like being mean and nasty to people. My grandmother was a witch. Then my mother, and she's just retired so I got the job. And I can do magic, but I just don't like to be horrible to people. It's so . . . horrible.'

She stood looking miserable.

'So I had to take over from my mother anyway, and move in here. She's gone to live in a nice house by the sea somewhere sunny.'

'But all the animals in the forest are terrified of you. They all told us to go home and stay away. And that . . . Tipsy . . . was a terrifying beast.'

'I told the animals to say that. Because . . . I'm scared. This forest is frightful and frightening and if people knew I was young and don't like being mean and my monster is a fluffy white kitten . . . Don't you know there are mean things out there? Like trolls?'

Raven Boy and Elf Girl looked at each other.

'We do,' said Raven Boy. 'But listen. You say you can do magic? Proper magic? Because we came here looking for help. You're supposed to be the Witch Who Knows Everything, right?'

'Well, yes,' said the witch, 'but it's more of a name than an actual job description.'

'Oh nuts,' said Elf Girl. 'Big hairy

monkey nuts.'

'Wait, Elf Girl,' said Raven Boy. 'Give her a chance. Witch, do you, er, have a name?'

The witch hesitated.

Then she mumbled something.

'Pardon me?' said Elf Girl.

'Florence,' said the witch, quietly.

'Florence?!' said Raven Boy.

'See? I don't even have a scary name. I'm a rubbish witch.'

'But supposing we gave you a chance to use your magic? To do something good, not something nasty?'

Florence lifted her head.

'Really?' she said. 'You know of such a thing?'

Elf Girl and Raven Boy smiled.

'With your magic,' cried Elf Girl, looking at them happily, 'and my mother's bow, and Raven Boy's strange and unfathomable ability to speak to small fluffy creatures, we can't fail!'

'Florence,' said Raven Boy, 'what do you know about ogres . . .?'

FIFTEEN

Elf Girl is a very good cook. She has a secret recipe for roasted beech-nut pie with wild strawberry jam.

The first thing they had to do was pull the swamp dog and Tipsy apart.

Once that was done, they set off back

through the swamp, while Florence explained about her family.

'Of course,' she was saying, 'my grandmother is the last of our family who we know actually ate children. Even my mother didn't do that, though I think she might once have nibbled a couple.'

Elf Girl and Raven Boy nodded politely, but they couldn't think how to reply to that.

It didn't matter, because Florence went on talking.

'So what are your names, anyway?'

'I'm Raven Boy!' said Raven Boy. 'I already told you that.'

'No, I mean, what are your real names?'

'It is my real name!' protested Raven Boy.

'It isn't,' said Elf Girl. 'But he won't tell me his real name. He says it begins with R but it's too embarrassing to mention.'

'I'm called Florence and I'm supposed to be a witch. I don't think you can have anything to worry about, no matter how silly your name is.'

'That's what I told him,' said Elf Girl.

'Because her name is even sillier than mine, her name is . . .'

And at this point Elf Girl whacked him so hard he fell off his feet.

She glared at him.

'I told you never to say it out loud!'

Raven Boy got to his feet, rubbing

the back of his head.

'That hurt,' he complained.

Florence the witch watched quietly.

'Is that really a magic bow?' she asked, changing the subject. 'Or just a stick?'

'It is a magic bow,' said Elf Girl. 'It's my mum's magic bow.'

'So why don't you just use it to zap the ogre who's destroying the forest, and be done with it?'

'I would, only my parents are missing and we think the ogre has something to do with it, so if I zap him, we won't be able to find out where they are.'

'Yes,' said Raven Boy. 'That plus the fact that she's totally useless with it.'

He stepped back quickly in case Elf Girl whacked him again.

Florence looked at the bow.

'It's a very nice stick. I mean bow,' she said. 'How does it work?'

'That's the problem,' explained Elf Girl. 'I'm not sure. My mum was going to explain all about it. I can sort of make it do some things, sometimes. And Raven Boy would have been troll food by now without it. It's just that it's

164

not exactly . . . reliable.'

'Maybe I can help!' cried Florence. 'I might be able to work it out, by magic. There are probably some words you have to use with it.'

'So are you really good at magic then?' asked Raven Boy.

Florence the witch hesitated.

'I'm . . . getting better,' she said.

'And what you said before, about the knowing everything bit. That's not exactly true either then?'

Florence the witch hesitated some more.

'No,' she said, staring at her feet. Then she perked up. 'But I do know one or two spells for finding things out! We could try them!'

'Really?' asked Elf Girl. 'Are you sure they work?'

'Absolutely.'

'Well, then,' said Elf Girl. 'There's something I need to know. I need to know if my family are still alive.'

She looked so worried and sad that Raven Boy felt a lump in his throat. He squeezed her hand, quickly.

'Could you find that out?' he asked Florence.

'Uh-huh,' she said. 'All I need is something that belongs to one of them.'

'I have the bow. Would that work?'

By now Elf Girl was looking very glum indeed.

Florence smiled.

'Sit down here with me. Hold the bow in the one hand, and my hand in the other. Think hard about your mum. That might help.'

Might? thought Raven Boy, but he didn't say anything as he didn't think it would make things any better.

Elf Girl and Florence sat down, and then Florence started acting weird, mumbling silly words with her eyes shut, and rocking backwards and forwards.

Elf Girl caught Raven Boy's eye, but he urged her to concentrate, and he and Rat backed away a few steps, and waited for the mumbling to stop.

The mumbling went on and on and on, and before too long, Raven Boy and Rat sat down too, feeling tired.

Raven Boy looked at the sky between the leaves of the trees, and began to worry. It would be dark soon, and for all they knew those trolls were close by and still hungry.

Suddenly, Florence jumped to her feet.

'I see them!' she cried, her eyes still shut. 'Your dad's tiny and your mum's tiny and they're both skinny and have blonde hair and then there's someone who could be your aunt, she looks very like your baby sister, and maybe that's your uncle, he's a bit fatter and I think that must be your mum's mum, she's old and quite little, but she looks like your mum.'

'That's them! That's them!' cried Elf Girl. 'Are they okay? Where are they?'

'They're okay,' she said. 'But they're scared. I can't tell where they are. It's dark and they're chained up in a cage or something.'

'We have to hurry! We have to help

them! There must be some way of knowing where they are . . .?'

Florence suddenly opened her eyes.

'Oh!' she said.

'Oh? What? Oh?'

'I mean,' explained Florence, 'right at the end there, I saw something that looked very much like a large foot come into the picture. The sort of foot that was so big it can only be . . .'

'. . . an ogre's?' asked Raven Boy.

Florence nodded.

Elf Girl jumped to her feet.

'That filthy ogre has them locked up somewhere! Come on! Now we know what to do, we go and sort out that smelly ogre and get him to let them go!'

With that she stomped off into the trees, not even knowing if she was going the right way, and too upset to care.

'Come on,' said Raven Boy. 'We'd better not lose her. At least they're still in one piece.'

'But Raven Boy,' said Florence. 'My magic might not have worked properly. For all I know, that was the past we

168

were looking at, not the present. They might already...'

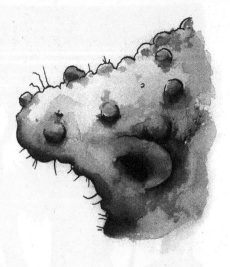

'Don't say it!' said Raven Boy. 'It would break Elf Girl's heart. We have to do our best. And hope.'

They skittered after Elf Girl, as the trees closed around them, night fell, and as, not very far away at all, a big warty troll nose sniffed the air.

'They was 'ere. I can smell 'em,' said the little troll.

SIXTEEN

Florence the witch's mother was very famous, possibly the wickedest, witchiest witch ever to live in Fright Forest.

Raven Boy, Elf Girl, Florence the witch and Rat crept through the forest.

They'd started off in a rush, but soon came to the conclusion that they didn't know where they were, or where they were going, and it was too dark to work it out.

Raven Boy looked for some small creature to speak to, but couldn't even find so much as a caterpillar.

'I have to find something soon,' he said.

'And what do we do till then?' asked Elf Girl. She looked into the inky blackness. 'This part of the forest is scary.'

'Scarier than the rest of it?' asked Raven Boy. 'Florence, don't you know it? We can't be that far from your hut?'

Florence shook her head.

'No. I don't. I always try and stay close to home. I told you. I'm not a scary witch, I'm a scared one.'

'So what do we do?'

Raven Boy frowned, and picked a feather from his hair. No matter how many he picked, there always seemed to be more.

'We're going to have to stay here and go on in the morning,' he said.

Elf Girl was not happy.

'But it's not safe. And I definitely don't want to spend the night in a tree again. I didn't sleep a wink!'

'Perhaps I can do something,' suggested Florence. 'I know a spell to protect us.'

'Will it make us invisible?' asked Elf Girl.

'No, not really. It just means we'll be less likely to be noticed. We'll be safe enough unless someone falls right on top of us.'

'You don't have a spell,' asked Raven Boy, 'to make some nice warm bread and cheese? Do you?'

'Sorry, ravenous boy, I don't.'

'Ha! I like that,' said Elf Girl. 'Ravenous Boy. That's a good one.'

'Elf Girl,' said Raven Boy. 'Shut up, will you?'

'Well, if you won't tell me your real name . . .' she began.

'Yes, so it begins with R, does it?' asked Florence.

'Oh no, not you too,' moaned Raven Boy. 'Just cast your spell and then we can all get some rest. Okay? Things will look much better in the morning.'

So Florence the witch wove her

spell, and though things didn't look or feel any different, they settled down, nestled in a big bank of leaves between the huge roots at the foot of a tall oak tree, and actually, they were almost invisible.

Which was just as well, because in the middle of the night, fortunately at one of the rare moments when Raven Boy was not snoring, the three trolls walked right past them.

Things did look better in the morning.

It was a bright and sunny day and Raven Boy found a large eagle to talk to. While he was doing that, Florence and Elf Girl managed to find enough wild strawberries and blueberries to take the worst of their hunger away.

Raven Boy came back.

'Oh, those eagles,' he was saying. 'They look so tough, but they're a bunch of jokers really. Did you know ...'

'Raven Boy!' said Elf Girl sternly. 'What did you find out?'

'Well, I was coming to that. My eagle pal had a good climb up into the sky, and he said we have to head east. That's where the sun's coming up.'

'I know that,' snapped Elf Girl. 'Why does he say that?'

'Well, because he can see vast chunks of the forest are missing over there.'

'Oh.'

'And he can see a big dirty ogre pulling them down. If your family's being held prisoner, they must be over there somewhere.'

Raven Boy pointed east, vaguely.

'But how far away are they?'

'About two days' walk.'

'Two days!' wailed Elf Girl. 'We can't take two days. We have to think of something faster.'

'I was coming to that too,' said Raven Boy. 'You see, there's that river we crossed before. It's not far from here and runs all the way there. If we could just find a boat or something, we could be there by this afternoon.'

'But how are we going to find a boat?'

'My eagle-eyed friend is looking for us. He told us to start walking towards the river and when he finds one, he's going to let me know.'

Elf Girl jumped up and down.

'Raven Boy! You're brilliant.'

Raven Boy nodded, smiling.

'Yes,' he said, 'yes, I am pretty cool, really.'

'Sometimes,' added Elf Girl, because she didn't want him to get too big-headed.

SEVENTEEN

Like ogres, trolls also eat anything, chewy or not, but they're less hungry in the daytime, when they're in human form.

They were barely at the river before the eagle swooped overhead, calling to

181

them.

Raven Boy looked up and waved, and the eagle soared away and off towards a distant mountain range.

'So?' asked Elf Girl.

'Elf Girl,' said Raven Boy, 'I know you find this hard to believe, but trust me. The eagle said there's a boat moored down the river by a collapsed bridge. All we need to do is borrow it, and off we go.'

Elf Girl still looked doubtful, but to her irritation Florence seemed to have no problem at all with the fact that Raven Boy had had a conversation with a bird of prey nearly as big as him.

Rat seemed in a very good mood, and sat on Raven Boy's head squeaking merrily until they arrived at the collapsed bridge.

'That's not a boat!' cried Elf Girl. 'It would be fairer to call it a jam jar.'

'It is a bit small,' said Florence, 'for three.'

Rat squeaked.

'Four,' Raven Boy said. 'Yes, I know. But it will have to do.'

The boat was tiny, and looked rather old and beaten up too, and it was no surprise that someone had left it by the old bridge to rot.

'Does it have oars?' asked Elf Girl.

'One. Sort of,' said Raven Boy, climbing in and holding up a pole.

'That's not an oar. It's a pole.'

'Well, it will have to do. The current is fast, we'll just need to steer from time to time.'

They climbed aboard, and the boat sank horribly close to the water line.

'Is this a great idea?' asked Florence. 'Actually?'

Elf Girl had that expression on her face again, the one where she looked very determined and sad all at the same time.

'It's fine,' said Raven Boy, as a big slop of water lapped over the side and into the bottom of the boat. 'Let's go!'

And off they went. Speedily.

Soon they had been dragged out into the centre of the river where the current was strongest and found themselves zipping along faster than they could have believed possible.

'We'll be there in no time!' cried Raven Boy.

'Or drowned!' wailed Florence, who wasn't enjoying it much.

Rat was enjoying it even less, and had hidden inside Raven Boy's shirt somewhere, and refused to come out, even to wave at a family of otters on

184

the riverbank.

By the time they should have been having lunch, none of them were enjoying it at all.

It was Elf Girl who noticed it first.

'Should our feet be wet?' she said.

'Hmm?' said Raven Boy, who had worked out how to steer the boat by dragging the pole in the water behind them at different angles. 'Did you say something?'

'Yes. I said, should our feet be wet? Soaking wet?'

Then they all noticed that there was a lot of water coming into the boat, through the bottom.

'Eeep!' wailed Raven Boy. 'We're sinking!'

'Never mind that!' cried Florence, who was sitting at the front.

'What do you mean, never mind? We could sink any second!'

'I think that's very likely, as it happens,' shouted Florence. 'Look!'

Florence had seen what none of the others had, that the river was about to stop.

About to stop in the way that rivers

do when they go over a waterfall.

They all screamed at once, but there was nothing else they could do, because the river was so strong, and they were travelling so fast.

'I can't swim!' was the last thing Raven Boy shouted as their tiny boat tipped over the edge of the waterfall.

Rat squeaked just to make sure they all knew he couldn't swim either, and then they were gone.

It seemed as if they were falling forever, though it only took a second or three before they sploshed into a lake below the waterfall.

Elf Girl surfaced first and dragged Raven Boy by the neck towards the bank. Florence seemed to be coping quite well, but Rat was nowhere to be seen. Then he popped up out of the water for a moment, and Florence grabbed him and sat him on her head.

They struggled to the bank choking

and spluttering, when suddenly, the sun went out.

Or rather, something got in the way of it.

They all looked up and screamed again, and then fainted.

Looking down at them was a very large, ugly and frankly terrifying ogre, with a tree in one hand and a sack in the other.

EIGHTEEN

**The magic in Elf Girl's mother's bow
is very old and mysterious, which
means it's different for everyone
who uses it.**

When they woke up again, they found
themselves in a pretty pickle.

191

They were in a cage, made of branches roughly lashed together. It was a tight squeeze, and they could barely move.

Raven Boy twisted his head and viewed the scene.

They were on an open piece of ground, a valley. Then Raven Boy realised it was open ground because the ogre had pulled up nearly every tree in sight. He twisted his head some more and saw that the cage they were crammed in was sitting on the deck of an enormous barge, floating on the lake into which they'd fallen.

Then he heard voices.

'Look! That one's moving!'

'He's alive . . . Maybe the others are too!'

Turning his head further still, Raven Boy saw that theirs was not the only cage on the deck. There were others, lots of others, and then he saw piles and piles of tree trunks on the barge, and then he saw that there was more than one barge.

'Hey!' a voice called to him. 'Hey, young fellah. Can you hear me?'

Raven Boy thought his head might fall off, he was turning it so far, but now he saw where the voice came from.

In the cage next to theirs was another group of people. There was something familiar about them, and Raven Boy knew why.

There was a thin man, and a thinner woman, and an older woman. All three

were tiny and blonde.

The man spoke.

'Hey! Is that . . .? It is! She's alive! She's alive!'

'Are you Elf Girl's parents?' Raven Boy asked.

'Who's Elf Girl?' asked the man.

'Sorry yes, I mean are you *her* parents?'

He nodded at Elf Girl.

'Yes! We thought the ogre had

194

eaten her!'

They were overjoyed and began to weep with happiness.

Elf Girl started to come round, and as soon as she had twisted herself out from underneath Raven Boy, she saw her parents waving and smiling at her.

'Mum! Dad! Granny! Is Cicely all right? And the others?'

'Yes, dear,' said her mum. 'They're all in other cages further along the deck.'

'What's going on? What are all these boats for? And the trees?'

'We don't know,' said Elf Girl's dad. 'The ogre has been piling up the boats for days with trees, and putting everyone he finds into cages. We think he's about to go on a long journey, but we don't know where, or why.'

'Aren't you going to introduce your friends?' asked Elf Girl's mum, in that way mums do.

'Oh, yes, well, this is . . . er . . . this is Raven Boy.'

Elf Girl's mum and dad exchanged looks, but they were both too nice to say anything.

195

'And this is Florence. She's a terrible witch.'

Florence came round as she heard her name.

'Hello,' she said.

'She doesn't seem that terrible,' said Elf Girl's mum.

'No, I mean she's a terrible witch. Just awful. Although, she did help us find you. But now we need to escape. We must do something!'

'We've been saying the same thing,' said Elf Girl's dad. 'But what can we do? We're locked in these cages, they're too small to wriggle out of, and your mum has lost her magic bow . . .'

'It's over there,' said Elf Girl, sounding miserable and scared all at once. 'The ogre seems to be using it as a toothpick.'

It was true. The ogre sat a good way off, leaning back against one of the few tall trees he hadn't pulled up yet, and, as far as Elf Girl could see, he was using her mother's magic bow to clean the gaps between his teeth.

'What's he been eating?' whispered Florence, horrified.

'Best not to think about it,' said Raven Boy. 'Right, it's time we came up with a plan.'

'Brave talk, lad,' said Elf Girl's dad. 'But what can we do? We've tried everything we could think of already.'

'Maybe so,' said Raven Boy with a glint in his eye, 'but then you didn't have a girl with a magic bow, a witch and a sneaky sniffy little rat with you.'

Everyone in the other cage looked blank, and then Rat appeared, running along the shore, jumping onto the mooring rope of the barge, and scampering up it till he perched on top of Raven Boy's head.

'Rat, old friend, the first thing we need is these ropes chewing.'

Raven Boy nodded at their hands, and the ropes that were tying the cage door shut.

'That's a lot of chewing,' said Elf Girl doubtfully.

But Rat didn't even waste time squeaking, and within a few moments Raven Boy's hands were free. While he set about untying his feet, Rat moved

on to the ropes binding the others.

'But what will we do then?' said Elf Girl's grandmother. 'That ogre's the size of a small hill!'

'That's where our witch comes in,' said Raven Boy. 'And we're going to get the bow back, and then . . .'

'And then . . .?'

'I haven't worked that bit out yet,' Raven Boy admitted.

'Well, whatever it is,' yelled Elf Girl, 'you'd better do it quickly! He's seen us!'

That was also true. Even as she spoke, the great big ogre lurched to his feet, and lumbered towards them.

Everyone screamed.

NINETEEN

Rat is pretty sure that Raven Boy and Elf Girl can't manage without him. They're a big responsibility, but he'll look after them.

Raven Boy pointed.
'Look! He's dropped his toothpick, I

mean the bow. Florence, can't you do something? Then Elf Girl can get the bow.'

'Which my dear mother never taught me to use properly!' cried Elf Girl.

'I'm sorry,' said her mum, 'but the thing is, the bow works differently for everyone. You'll have to find out for yourself how it works for you. It's yours now, I'm giving it to you.'

'Oh wonderful. Couldn't you have waited till my birthday?' Elf Girl wailed.

By now the three were climbing out of their cage, and Rat was starting on the next one.

'Quick!' someone shouted.

'He's coming!' shouted someone else.

'Don't rush me!' shouted Florence. 'There's one thing I could try, I suppose.'

She shut her eyes and began to mumble and move her hands in strange ways.

'Hurry!' whispered Raven Boy, remembering how long Florence's last lot of spell mumbling had taken, and watching the ogre getting closer. 'If he gets here, we're going to be dessert.'

Florence mumbled some more, and then opened her eyes.

'That's it,' she said. 'Finished.'

'That's what, exactly?' cried Raven Boy, and then he added, 'Run!'

The ogre had reached the barge, and everyone who had been freed jumped onto the shore, or into the lake. Those who hit the ground began running wildly, and for a moment the ogre was confused, swiping here and there at the tiny people darting between his legs.

'Florence! What did you do? Try again! Try anything!'

But Florence was busy running too.

Then, from out of nowhere, it began to get foggy. Seriously foggy, so all that they could see of the ogre was about as far up as his knees.

'Florence!' cried Raven Boy. 'You did it! Elf Girl, get the bow! Zap him!'

Elf Girl didn't need telling twice, and was stumbling off into the fog towards where she'd last seen the bow.

It was chaos. Everyone was running

around madly, trying to avoid the ogre's feet because he was now stomping and whirling in an effort to catch someone. From somewhere in the fog, Elf Girl called, 'I can't find it!' and from somewhere else, Raven Boy

screamed, 'Look harder!'
And then Elf Girl shouted, 'Aha!'

There was a long pause then, as Elf Girl tried to work out what it was she didn't understand about her bow.

A blinding flash lit up the fog like a blanket of light, and the ogre stopped in his tracks.

For a fraction of a second it was eerily silent, and then someone yelled, 'Move!' because the ogre was starting to fall.

He hit the ground with a terrific thud that made the earth shake, and he lay still.

The fog began to lift as everyone crept towards the figure of the ogre lying on the grass.

Raven Boy noticed it first.

'He's . . . he's sleeping! Elf Girl, you put him to sleep!'

Elf Girl smiled.

'Did you mean to do that?' asked Florence.

Elf Girl shook her head.

'I'm not sure,' she said. 'Yes, maybe.'

'Who cares?'

'But how long will he sleep for?' asked Florence.

'Good point!' cried Raven Boy. 'Get

the ropes from the boat. We have to tie
him up.'

So they did.

TWENTY

Trolls are very whiffy indeed, and can sometimes capture their victims by smell alone.

Then the ogre woke up, he found himself not only trussed up with a couple of hundred ropes, he found

209

himself tied to the tree he'd been leaning against earlier.

He also found himself confronted by the several dozen people he'd taken prisoner as he'd uprooted the trees in their forest.

They weren't happy.

'Can you talk?' said Raven Boy, folding his arms and trying to look very fierce, though in fact his knees were shaking.

Suddenly, the ogre roared at them all. 'RAAAH.'

A couple of people fainted. Raven Boy didn't, but his knees knocked so badly he could hear them.

'Now stop that!' said Raven Boy, looking nervous as the ogre pulled and struggled against the ropes.

'Or you'll do what?' snarled the ogre. 'I'm going to eat every last one of you!'

'So, you can talk.'

'Of course I can talk,' the ogre growled, in a very deep voice.

'Hah!' said Raven Boy. Then he couldn't think of anything smarter to say, so he let Elf Girl take over.

'We were just trying to decide what

to do with you! But letting you go was not on our list. So far we have drowning, beheading, locking you up for ever, and throwing away the key. You've ruined our forest, and you've eaten people, and we're very angry with you.'

The ogre just roared again. 'RAAAH.'

And a few more people fainted.

'I'm going to eat you so hard it's going to really hurt!' he cried.

He tugged and strained some more at the ropes. One of them snapped, and the ogre had a mighty hand free. He began swiping at the people standing closest to him, and when they ran away, he started to tug at the rest of the ropes instead.

'Right!' said Elf Girl. 'I've had about enough of this.'

She grabbed her bow.

'What are you going to do?' asked Raven Boy.

'Just watch!'

She aimed her bow at the ogre's nose and Raven Boy noticed that her arrow-shaped birthmark was glowing brightly. Though there was still no real string to the bow, a glowing line appeared in the air, which suddenly twanged as Elf Girl let go.

The ogre, who had been straining at the ropes, jumped as if he'd been stung by a hundred wasps.

'Oh,' he said, suddenly sounding very different. Not angry at all any more,

but quiet. Meek. Timid.

'Now,' cried Elf Girl, 'just you start behaving nicely.'

'Yes,' said the ogre. 'All right. Sorry.'

'Elf Girl!' cried Raven Boy. 'What have you done?'

'I have knocked some niceness into him.'

'Hah! You did it! You knew what you were doing!'

'Yes,' said Elf Girl. 'I think so . . .'

But Raven Boy wasn't listening. He'd walked right up to the ogre and was staring into his face.

'You are a very bad ogre. You've eaten lots of people and pulled up lots of trees.'

'I haven't eaten anyone for days,' the ogre said.

'We saw you! Just now, when you were sitting here!'

'That was a badger,' the ogre said. 'I don't eat people. Often.'

'Well, all right, but what about the trees?' cried Florence. 'Half the forest is missing!'

The ogre looked sorry.

'Well, I did do that,' he said. 'But it's

not my fault.'

'Not your fault?' cried Raven Boy. 'You pulled them up with your bare hands.'

'I mean,' said the ogre, 'I know I did it, but I was told to do it.'

'You! Made to do something! I don't believe it!'

Raven Boy scratched his head.

'Who made you do it?'

Now the ogre looked scared. They couldn't believe it, but he was trembling.

'I don't want to say his name out loud,' he said finally.

'Who?'

'The one who made me do it. He told me to come here and tear the forest down, and take everyone as slaves and send them and the trees back to him.'

Everyone began muttering at once. Raven Boy whispered to the ogre.

'But who?'

And, looking around him nervously, as if checking to see who was listening, the ogre whispered back.

'The Goblin King.'

'Who's the Goblin King?' asked Elf Girl.

'Shh!' cried the ogre. 'Not so loud! If he hears you, you'll be in trouble.'

'But who is he?'

'If you've never heard of him, you'll wish you never had.'

'That doesn't make sense,' said Raven Boy.

'Well, I mean once you've heard of him, you'll wish you never had. He's the most evil, terrifying creature that ever lived. He rules a land far away from here, but he wants to take over everything, destroy everything. And be mean to everyone.'

'But why?' asked Elf Girl.

'I don't know. He just does,' said the ogre, 'and he made me start on the forest here. He wants the trees for firewood, and the people for slaves. And he's not going to stop until he's taken over the whole world.'

There was a lot of shaking of heads and muttering.

'Well, that's terrible,' said Elf Girl after a while.

'Agreed,' said Raven Boy. 'We have to do something about it. We have to stop him.'

Now everyone began muttering at once.

'You can't defeat the Goblin King!' someone said. 'He's pure evil.'

'You hadn't even heard of him a minute ago!' said Raven Boy. 'And five minutes before that, you wouldn't have said we could defeat this chap either, would you? But we did! And someone has to stop this Goblin King. Ogre, I'll make you a deal.'

The ogre looked up.

'What?' he said.

'If we let you go, you have to promise to come and help us defeat the Goblin King.'

'If you let me go,' said the ogre, 'I'm running away as far as I can. Sorry, but you don't know how vicious and mean and evil and . . .'

'Yes! Okay!' cried Raven Boy. 'We get the idea. Okay, look, I'll do you another deal. If we let you go, you have to promise not to eat anyone, to stop tearing up the forest, and you have to promise to help replant trees and rebuild people's houses. Then you can run away. Okay?'

The ogre thought about this for a long time, then he nodded.

'Okay,' he said.

'Raven Boy,' said Elf Girl, 'are you sure that's a good idea?'

The ogre heard her.

'Oh, don't worry. Ogres always tell the truth. We might be big and mean but we never lie. I'll help rebuild everyone's homes, and then I'm running. If I were you, I'd do the same thing.'

Raven Boy looked at the ogre fiercely.

'Never! We're going to go and give that Goblin King what for. Right?'

With a flourish of his coat tails he turned to the crowd, waiting for a cheer that didn't come.

People stared at their toes and some began to shuffle away.

'Right?' cried Raven Boy again.

No one looked him in the eye.

'The thing is,' someone said, 'it

219

sounds a bit dangerous. And I'm really busy at the moment. Got lots on.'

'Yes, me too,' said another voice. 'Busy weekend.'

The shuffling continued.

'Isn't there anyone who cares enough about the world to come with me?' asked Raven Boy, but he didn't sound dramatic any more, he sounded defeated.

Then, there was a squeak, and Rat jumped onto his head. He squeaked again.

'Thanks, Rat,' said Raven Boy, smiling. He looked at Elf Girl.

'Elf Girl?' he said. 'How about you? We make quite a team.'

Elf Girl looked worried. Then she looked at her parents, and her family, and then back at Raven Boy.

She grinned.

'Of course I'll come with you!'

'No!' cried her parents. 'No, you can't. It's too dangerous.'

'But someone has to do something,' she said. 'And you have to stay and look after Granny and Cicely. But me and my bow have to save the world, with Raven Boy!'

Raven Boy laughed.

'We're going to save the world, so remember our names. Raven Boy and Elf Girl.'

'Elf Girl and Raven Boy,' said Elf Girl.

'No, Raven Boy and Elf Girl.'

'Elf Girl and Raven Boy.'

'Maybe if you're going to save the world, you should save your breath first,' said Florence.

Rat squeaked, and everyone laughed.

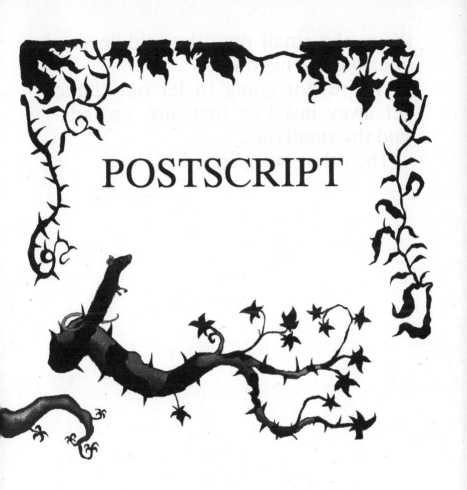

POSTSCRIPT

Yes, everyone laughed, even the ogre, and even the three men standing at the back of the group, a little way away from everyone else.

And as Raven Boy and Elf Girl made their preparations to go in search of the evil Goblin King, and said their goodbyes, the three men watched

223

them; the small one, the middle-sized one, and the big one.

'We're not going to let our dinner get away just like that, are we lads?' said the small one.

The other two grinned.